Acting Edition

Jane Austen's Lady Susan

by Rob Urbinati

I0589011

‖SAMUEL FRENCH‖

A staged reading of *JANE AUSTEN'S LADY SUSAN* was presented at Western Oregon University in Salem, Oregon (David Janowiak, Division Chair) on December 1, 2018 under the direction of Ted deChatalet. The The cast was as follows:

LADY SUSAN	Becky Bond
FREDERICA	Selena Moreno
CHARLES VERNON	Gabe Elmore
CATHERINE VERNON	Stephanie Kintz
REGINALD DE COURCY	Hunter Atkin
ALICIA JOHNSON	Phoebe Thompson
SIR JAMES MARTIN	Lawrence Dannen

A staged reading of *JANE AUSTEN'S LADY SUSAN* was subsequently presented at Invisible Dog Art Center in Brooklyn, New York (Lucien Zayan, Founder and Director) on April 22, 2019 under the direction of the author. The cast was as follows:

LADY SUSAN	Adrianna Dufay
FREDERICA	Marielle Renée Rousseau
CHARLES VERNON	Donal Brophy
CATHERINE VERNON	Salomé M. Krell
REGINALD DE COURCY	Jeremy Beck
ALICIA JOHNSON	Patricia Randell
SIR JAMES MARTIN	Kevin Sebastian

A staged reading of *JANE AUSTEN'S LADY SUSAN* was subsequently presented at Stageworks Theatre in Houston, Texas (Michael Montgomery, Artistic Director) on August 31, 2019 under the direction of Lisa Garza. The cast was as follows:

LADY SUSAN	Melissa Renthrop
FREDERICA	Alexis Bounds
CHARLES VERNON	J. Blanchard
CATHERINE VERNON	Casey Radle
REGINALD DE COURCY	Daniel Casse
ALICIA JOHNSON	Ellen Michaels
SIR JAMES MARTIN	Justin Finch

CHARACTERS

LADY SUSAN – Thirties. A handsome, manipulative widow.

FREDERICA – Teens. Lady Susan's clever, guileless daughter.

CHARLES VERNON – Thirties, Lady Susan's patient, obliging brother-in-law.

CATHERINE VERNON – Twenties. Charles Vernon's suspicious wife.

REGINALD DE COURCY – Twenties. Catherine Vernon's dashing younger brother.

ALICIA JOHNSON – Older. Lady Susan's chatty confidante.

SIR JAMES MARTIN – Any age. Wealthy, dimwitted (possibly overweight) bachelor.

SETTING

The events transpire over the course of a week in a single location – the Drawing Room of Charles and Catherine Vernon's Estate at Churchill, in England. The house is a good one, and everything announces plenty and elegance (or at least some think so).

TIME

May 1800.

AUTHOR'S NOTES

– The Drawing Room should have at least two entrances, on opposite sides of the stage.

– All of the actors can be older than the ages suggested, but the differences between their ages should remain the same.

– "Papa" and "Mama" should be pronounced with the accent on the last syllable.

Dramaturgy
Adrianna Dufay

About The Dream Board

JANE AUSTEN'S LADY SUSAN takes place on a Unit Set, but the action covers a week in time, and the characters would necessarily change clothing. There are simple, quick and cost-efficient ways to give the appearance of different costumes, without a full change.

A neutral "under-layer" can be worn by the female characters throughout an entire act, or the entire play. A simple Empire-Waist Gown is an example of such an under-layer. When an actor wearing this under-layer requires a different costume, she can add a jacket, vest, over-skirt, shawl or hat. Also, a low-necked, short-sleeved evening gown can become a day-dress by adding a high-necked jacket. Collars, yokes and jewelry which can be added and removed with snaps or Velcro are also useful. All of these adjustments can be done when there are "quick-changes," and will provide the illusion of a complete change in attire for audiences.

The male characters in *JANE AUSTEN'S LADY SUSAN* wear period suits, which can be varied by adding various vests and neckwear, such as cravats, bow-ties, and neckties.

Sharon Sobel

ACT I
MONDAY

Scene One
Afternoon

LADY SUSAN. It is a delight to meet you, Mrs Vernon. Your home is a jewel, and the furnishings exquisite.

CATHERINE. That is most kind, Lady Susan – and very astute.

LADY SUSAN. My dearest Charles, I am indebted to you for your invitation. I have longed to spend some weeks in Churchill, and am sure to profit from your company.

CATHERINE. Some weeks, is it? How generous of you, husband.

LADY SUSAN. Only if it is entirely convenient for you and Mr Vernon to receive me for that length of time.

CHARLES. Nothing would afford us more joy.

CATHERINE. I rather doubt that your appetite for diversion can be quenched as easily in Churchill as in town, Lady Susan.

LADY SUSAN. London was not at all what I was led to expect from the luminous watercolors in our drawing room at Vernon Castle. I grew weary of the drizzle and fog. All the while there, I pined for country air.

CATHERINE. Climate forced your retreat, you say? I heard reports that you had become quite the center of attention in the first circle.

LADY SUSAN. The Manwarings urged me to prolong my stay, but their dispositions were too lively for my present circumstances. I am, after all, still in mourning.

CATHERINE. As one would hope.

CHARLES. I cannot imagine your sorrow, Susan. My brother was such a kind-hearted man.

LADY SUSAN. I doubt I shall ever fully recover. But my condition is sure to benefit from the calm of Churchill – and the companionship it offers.

CATHERINE. I am sorry to disappoint you, Lady Susan, but while Mr Vernon and I roll in money, we have no talent whatever for entertaining.

LADY SUSAN. Will I not have the good fortune to meet your father, the esteemed Sir Fitzwilliam de Courcy? He is a man to whom the great word "respectable" is always applied.

CATHERINE. Father is gravely ill and could not possibly journey from Parklands to pay a social call.

LADY SUSAN. This must be a challenging time, Mrs Vernon. You have all my heart.

CHARLES. Our son is attending Sir Fitzwilliam and Lady De Courcy –

CATHERINE. – until Charles and I are free to visit.

LADY SUSAN. I am loath to disturb you, dear lady. If you prefer, I could return to London and visit at a more suitable time.

CATHERINE. *(Pleased.)* A most generous offer.

CHARLES. Young Charles will provide all the comfort your parents need, dear wife.

LADY SUSAN. *(To* **CATHERINE.***)* Your brother is also admired, and frequently discussed in town.

CATHERINE. Alas, Reginald must remain at father's side in his time of need.

CHARLES. I trust it will be impossible for the lad to resist a chance to behold the renowned Lady Susan.

LADY SUSAN. How could I be of interest to such an impetuous young man?

CHARLES. *(Lightly.)* I see Mr De Courcy's reputation has found its way to London – although I'll wager the word "respectable" is more frequently applied to father than to son.

CATHERINE. Tush, Charles. My brother allows himself a certain amount of flirting, but always within the bounds of what is appropriate. And with women of his age.

LADY SUSAN. *(Lightly.)* As one would hope. But young men are often surprisingly susceptible.

CATHERINE. I fear we shall be entirely devoid of company to amuse you during your stay.

LADY SUSAN. Want of distraction will provide the ideal occasion to renew my friendship with you, Charles – and at long last, to become known to your dear wife.

CATHERINE. That is considerate, Lady Susan – and quite appropriate.

LADY SUSAN. How do you occupy yourselves, may I ask?

CATHERINE. Raising our son, of course.

CHARLES. And I have my banking-house.

LADY SUSAN. What do you do for leisure?

CHARLES. I read and hunt.

LADY SUSAN. *(Slyly, to CHARLES.)* Solitary occupations.

CATHERINE. Whilst I select furnishings for our home, and statuary for the gardens.

LADY SUSAN. The household is impeccable, Mrs Vernon. And I noticed when I arrived how – exhaustively the grounds were embellished.

CHARLES. I often wonder how my wife manages it. I have never seen her out-of-doors.

CATHERINE. I can assess the gardens quite satisfactorily from the windows in the breakfast-room, Charles. To appreciate nature does not require one to romp about the shrubbery.

LADY SUSAN. I applaud your partiality for the common places of existence.

CATHERINE. Mr Vernon and I find solace in tranquility – and clean living.

CHARLES. Frederica appeared sallow and withdrawn at the funeral. I hoped she would accompany you to Churchill, where the country breezes might prove hospitable.

CATHERINE. Poor girl, to have her father seized at so young an age.

LADY SUSAN. Moreover, the sudden demise of Mr Vernon has kept me from providing Frederica the attention which duty and devotion demand.

CHARLES. You mustn't reprove yourself, after all you have endured. Is she with a guardian in town?

LADY SUSAN. Mrs Johnson is preoccupied with her husband, who is laid low with the gout. Regretfully, I was forced to separate from my daughter. I placed Frederica at Miss Summer's school on my way hither.

CHARLES. Girls of the best families attend Miss Summer's. My niece should make useful connections there.

LADY SUSAN. My intention exactly, although the price is immense, and beyond what I can expend for any length of time.

CHARLES. Fear not. I shall make the necessary arrangements for Frederica to stay as long as you desire.

LADY SUSAN. You are too generous, Charles.

CATHERINE. Indeed, Mr Vernon's generosity is without restraint.

LADY SUSAN. A trait he shares with Frederick. I wish so that you had chosen to make my husband's acquaintance, dear lady.

CATHERINE. I trust that Frederica has inherited all of her father's finest qualities.

LADY SUSAN. She has Frederick's decency, but few of his abilities. I should very much like for her to acquire an education. I was so much indulged in my youth that I am without the accomplishments considered necessary nowadays to finish a woman.

CHARLES. You undervalue your abilities.

CATHERINE. I for one do not endorse the prevailing fashion for women to indulge themselves with learning.

CHARLES. It will gain Frederica some attention, to be sure.

LADY SUSAN. And more importantly, a husband.

CATHERINE. A woman does not require any such skills to secure a husband. I wed one of the wealthiest men in England with no skills whatever.

LADY SUSAN. Given our fragile position, I must ensure that my daughter's talents are fully developed.

CATHERINE. Lady Susan, I do not flatter to suggest that you are extravagantly qualified to acquire a suitable spouse for Frederica. I supposed you fixed in London for just such a purpose.

LADY SUSAN. I can only advise and encourage. My daughter possesses an independent spirit.

CHARLES. As does our Charles. Six years of age, and he has already begun to display an interest in banking.

CATHERINE. And he possesses the most exquisite taste.

LADY SUSAN. A financier *and* an aesthete. The boy sounds miraculous. I am eager to hear more of this prodigy, but alas, I am weary from my travels and must look a fright.

CATHERINE. Your appearance is perfectly adequate. Stay a while longer. I am eager to learn the particulars of your recreations in town.

LADY SUSAN. I look forward to sharing confidences with you in the coming weeks, Mrs Vernon. Charles, might this evening, when I am refreshed, be an opportune time to discuss private matters?

CHARLES. Happily, my friend.

*(**LADY SUSAN** exits. After a few moments.)*

Lady Susan possesses an amiable spirit, does she not?

CATHERINE. She has recovered too hastily from the death of her husband.

CHARLES. You must permit that her address to you was gentle and affectionate.

CATHERINE. It was a cunning performance that had no affect on my cautious temper. But clearly, she has already played on your charitable nature.

CHARLES. She spoke of her daughter with deep concern.

CATHERINE. I fear for the girl's well-being, at the mercy of such an unprincipled mother. Is Frederica handsome, Charles?

CHARLES. Had you accompanied me to the funeral as I implored, you might have availed yourself of the opportunity to assess her features.

CATHERINE. Why did you neglect to consult me on such a weighty decision as inviting Lady Susan into our home?

CHARLES. To avoid your attempt to prevent it.

CATHERINE. My utmost desire was never to meet the wretched creature, and now you have thrust her upon me!

CHARLES. Why did you rush Charles off to Parklands while I was out hunting yesterday?

CATHERINE. To avoid your attempt to prevent it. I will not have our son corrupted by her influence.

CHARLES. I beg you, Catherine – set your ill will to one side.

CATHERINE. Precisely when did you extend this covert invitation?

CHARLES. As soon as I returned from the funeral.

CATHERINE. Three months past! Why did she dally so long before accepting your offer?

CHARLES. My invitation did not convey urgency.

CATHERINE. Concede it, Charles. You were forced to wait until she was expelled by Mrs Manwaring.

CHARLES. I rather doubt she was expelled, dear.

CATHERINE. The dissipated style of living in London is precisely suited to a woman of her proclivities. She would not have accepted your offer had she not been flung out.

CHARLES. That representation is as uncharitable as it is unfounded.

CATHERINE. Her tardy response and abrupt departure are proof certain that something objectionable transpired in town, which I shall unearth – and prove that she is ill-suited for our company.

CHARLES. Where there is a disposition to distrust, evidence will never be found wanting.

CATHERINE. Why did she stay so long in residence with the Manwarings, paraded about by the disreputable Alicia Johnson, if that manner of living did not suit her? I do not believe a word she utters.

CHARLES. Lady Susan is a widow, in need of our consolation.

CATHERINE. Now that she has laid siege to our home, I am convinced she will gain a purchase on your pliable disposition, and compel you to bestow an overly generous handling of Frederick's inheritance.

CHARLES. I shall discharge my obligation and assist his widow and child as my brother would have wished, had he lived to finalize his will.

CATHERINE. Alas, he did not, and thus the money and property she is provided is entirely at our discretion.

CHARLES. At my discretion.

CATHERINE. How irritating you are this morning. As always, in the face of abundant evidence to the contrary, you are stubbornly disposed to think the best of everyone.

CHARLES. I happily own to it.

CATHERINE. Lady Susan's sole purpose in marrying your brother was to lay claim to Vernon Castle. And now, with Frederick gone and –

CHARLES. *(Interrupting.)* Inheritance law requires that the Castle is bequeathed to Frederica when she weds.

CATHERINE. If she weds. From all reports, she is a plain girl, unworthy of attention, which accounts for her mother's drastic efforts in town.

CHARLES. Be charitable, Catherine, I beg you.

CATHERINE. Vernon Castle is in our possession now, Charles, and it shall belong to our son. But mark my words – the woman will employ all her powers to reclaim it!

CHARLES. Which powers, pray?

CATHERINE. Her talent to entice, which she has been advancing recklessly in town – and, may I add, without the advantage of youth, which is evident about the eyes and chin.

CHARLES. Susan has always possessed a rare union of beauty, intelligence and grace. She is not at all the seductress you portray.

CATHERINE. Her act of treachery before we were wed is a wound from which I still suffer. I shall never forgive her.

CHARLES. Which is why you have chosen to credit the reckless allegations of her behavior in town.

CATHERINE. The woman is morally unfit.

CHARLES. *(Takes her hands, gently.)* Mrs Vernon, in the six years since we wed, you have kept me from the companionship of my brother, and his dear wife and child. The time has come to make amends, and welcome Lady Susan into our family.

CATHERINE. When pigs fly!

Scene Two
Evening

LADY SUSAN. *(Lightly.)* Did you pose for any of the statuary in the garden, Charles? I noticed features similar to yours on one of the innumerable ancient Greeks.

CHARLES. Which features, pray?

LADY SUSAN. It would be immodest of me to elaborate.

CHARLES. Then elaborate you must!

(They laugh.)

I have missed you, dear friend.

LADY SUSAN. There is nothing I would not do for those who are *truly* my friends, Charles.

CHARLES. I too have no notion of loving people by halves. It is not my nature – although Mrs Vernon has put my conviction to the test.

LADY SUSAN. How illuminating to meet your wife, after all these years. May I speak candidly?

CHARLES. I expect nothing less.

LADY SUSAN. The woman is unskilled at disguising her true feelings toward me.

CHARLES. A trait inherited from her mother – the most tactless Gorgon in all England. Mercifully, Lady De Courcy will keep clear of Churchill whilst you are present.

LADY SUSAN. *(Lightly.)* I admire tactlessness in women – unless I am the target.

CHARLES. No doubt, as we speak, Catherine is writing her mother about your arrival. And while the old fossil will strenuously object, I'll wager Reginald shall sally in at any moment now.

LADY SUSAN. I presume he accepts Catherine's account of my wickedness?

CHARLES. Which will tempt him, no doubt.

LADY SUSAN. He will come into considerable wealth and property when his father passes. That surely has him besieged by the young ladies hereabouts.

CHARLES. Reginald is an eligible – indeed, an *extravagantly* eligible bachelor.

LADY SUSAN. *(Lightly.)* I should like to meet the man, if only to provoke his sister.

CHARLES. Susan, I invited you to Churchill to put an end to these quarrels.

LADY SUSAN. Without informing your wife, apparently. Dear Charles, I would never have attempted to discourage your marriage had I known it would cause such a rupture in our friendship.

CHARLES. You did what you thought best for me, as companion and confidante.

LADY SUSAN. Yet Mrs Vernon's behavior this afternoon aligns with my warnings.

CHARLES. I considered your appeal, then made my choice – for better or worse.

LADY SUSAN. It was she who discouraged you from visiting me and Frederick.

CHARLES. Prohibited, in point of fact.

LADY SUSAN. Six years, Charles! How could you yield to such a heartless petition?

CHARLES. To avoid conflict, which is my principal occupation in our marriage.

LADY SUSAN. The Charles I remember was of bolder fiber.

CHARLES. I behaved foolishly, Susan. And when I saw Frederica at the funeral, growing into womanhood,

I resolved to end this separation. And now – you are here!

LADY SUSAN. Living in the country at Vernon Castle, with Frederick and our daughter – those were blissful days. But to my surprise, I found London rather scintillating.

CHARLES. I prefer the country. Everyone in town is either overdressed or under-educated – or both.

LADY SUSAN. *(Amused.)* I shall strive to endure Churchill for a week or two, facilitated by your fond companionship. Please tell me you have not become tedious.

CHARLES. I promise to keep you amused, and to deflect Catherine's interrogatories.

LADY SUSAN. And I shall display my best behavior toward her. It will be one of my most challenging performances.

CHARLES. *(Takes her hand.)* Dear Susan – how have you been coping these months since my brother's death?

LADY SUSAN. When Frederick was taken ill, we all presumed a speedy recovery. He asked after you often, Charles. Then suddenly, he was gone. I have not slept a night since. *(Fighting tears.)* Frederica is despondent. They were inseparable – like Juno's swans. For her sake, I persevere. One must. To that end, I endeavored to occupy myself in town.

CHARLES. Which did not pass without notice.

LADY SUSAN. Oh, Charles – how can I be the mother she needs when I am tasked with providing for her until she weds? What if one of us is taken ill, like Frederick?

CHARLES. Before you depart, we will settle your inheritance. Trust that you and Frederica shall lack nothing.

LADY SUSAN. Dear friend, you have all of your brother's good nature, and his benevolent disposition. *(Amused.)* Is it true that you "roll in money"?

CHARLES. *(Lightly.)* Of course – as do all men who have their names on banking-houses.

LADY SUSAN. My worry is that Mrs Vernon might attempt to curb what your good nature would encourage you to provide.

CHARLES. The effort is afoot. But Catherine's chief interest is our son. Once she is assured that you have no claims on Vernon Castle, she will withdraw.

LADY SUSAN. No claims on the Castle? But where are am I to reside?

CHARLES. I will happily provide all the resources for you and my niece to settle anywhere you choose.

LADY SUSAN. You misunderstand, Charles. I ventured to London to find a husband for Frederica. My intention was to return to the Castle once my mission was achieved.

CHARLES. Catherine insists it be given to our son.

LADY SUSAN. My husband fully expected Vernon Castle to remain in my possession after his death.

CHARLES. Mrs Vernon is disinclined to yield, as you have witnessed.

LADY SUSAN. Then you must induce her, Charles. You owe it to the brother you deserted!

TUESDAY

Scene Three
Afternoon

REGINALD. Lady Susan, what brings a woman such as yourself to Churchill? It must seem insufferably dull after your escapades in London.

LADY SUSAN. I find the country quite soothing, actually. And your sister has been ever so gracious.

REGINALD. But it offers so little amusement – no music or dancing, *(Lightly.)* or men to snare into your web.

CHARLES. *(Lightly.)* Reginald, if you please.

CATHERINE. My brother and I are eager to learn more of your dalliances in town, Lady Susan.

REGINALD. Indeed, some of what I heard was quite audacious. I admire that in a woman!

LADY SUSAN. Since Frederick's passing, many false claims have been made about me. Such is the fate of a young widow.

REGINALD. Yet I think it extraordinary that so many accounts should find their way to my ears.

CHARLES. A journey expedited by my wife, no doubt.

CATHERINE. Am I not permitted to communicate with my own flesh and blood?

REGINALD. *(To* **LADY SUSAN.***)* When I first received dispatches of your bewitching powers, I thought, "What an enchantress she must be!" Now we are graced with the fount of these tales of conquest.

LADY SUSAN. I am not any such woman, Mr De Courcy. Rather quickly, I grew weary of the perpetual quest for diversion in town.

CHARLES. These "diversions" are no concern of ours here in Churchill.

CATHERINE. They concern me very much.

REGINALD. But Charles, if even a handful of the stories are true, her ladyship's powers of seduction must be extraordinary. As an emergent flirt, it will be instructive for me to observe her behavior.

LADY SUSAN. I shall disappoint you, Mr De Courcy. I am entirely unremarkable.

CATHERINE. Is it not true that Sir James was engaged to Miss Manwaring until you arrived at their home, whereupon he promptly detached himself from his intended?

REGINALD. Do tell!

CHARLES. Is Susan expected to counter every amplified conjecture?

LADY SUSAN. *(To* **REGINALD.***)* Perhaps you were provided with these fantastical tales to tickle your desire for scandal.

CATHERINE. My brother always confines himself to *decent* flirtation.

REGINALD. *Almost* always.

CATHERINE. Letters and hearsay can prove unreliable, Lady Susan. I am desperate to learn directly all that transpired in London since your husband's funeral.

LADY SUSAN. Your desperation does not go unnoticed, Mrs Vernon. On occasion in town, I sought opportunities for Frederica to display her distinctions. But more often than not, I kept to myself. I am, in fact, a private woman.

REGINALD. But a ravishing one, I must say!

CATHERINE. And apparently has been, these many years.

LADY SUSAN. *(Coyly.)* Reginald, your flattery is excessive this afternoon. I am unworthy of such buttery praise.

REGINALD. I, on the other hand, never tire of compliments! I presume you have received bulletins of my magnetism?

CATHERINE. *(To **LADY SUSAN**.)* And of his obedience, no doubt. Our dear parents are blessed with a devoted son – and given father's severe condition, I trust Reginald's steps shall soon be bent thither.

CHARLES. My dear Catherine, Sir Fitzwilliam does not require unremitting supervision.

REGINALD. In point of fact, my boldness unnerves mother and father. Since young Charles arrived, they have ignored me completely. I am certain they haven't a clue I've fled.

CATHERINE. Tush, Reginald. Mother watches your every move like a hawk.

CHARLES. She *is* rather a bird of prey.

CATHERINE. Lady De Courcy is doting, like myself, and like every proper materfamilias – which is why I was kept at her side, rather than catapulted into school like some young girls. I expect I shall receive a letter from her soon, lamenting your sudden departure.

CHARLES. She is wont to lamenting. It is one of her most frequent occupations, along with badgering. *(To **REGINALD**.)* Stay a while, my boy, and we shall hunt.

REGINALD. I should enjoy that, Charles. "The whirring pheasant springs, and mounts exulting on triumphant wings."

LADY SUSAN. How utterly charming, Mr De Courcy. Did you compose that verse?

REGINALD. Aha! Lady Susan has succumbed to my charm! But I must credit Alexander Pope: "The vivid green his

shining plumes unfold, *(He approaches* **LADY SUSAN.***)*
His painted wings and breast that flames with gold."

CATHERINE. That is quite enough, Reginald!

REGINALD. How long might we hope to enjoy your society in Churchill, Lady Susan?

LADY SUSAN. For as long as your sister will have me.

REGINALD. I relish the chance to dawdle with the most accomplished coquette in England!

CHARLES. My dear Susan, I apologize on behalf of this raffish lad. I assure you that beneath his preening self-confidence beats a tender heart.

LADY SUSAN. A dashing young man is easily forgiven – even a mischievous one.

REGINALD. There, you see! Her ladyship appreciates my candor, and is not in the least offended by my sauciness.

LADY SUSAN. I confess that I find him quite diverting, Charles.

CATHERINE. Whilst I consider his behavior reckless and overly familiar this afternoon.

LADY SUSAN. Do not temper his conduct for my sake, Mrs Vernon. I sense admiration even in his most brazen remarks.

REGINALD. You see straight through me, Lady Susan. I feel entirely exposed.

LADY SUSAN. Beware, lad – I have always taken exquisite pleasure in taming a bold spirit.

REGINALD. Is it your desire to tame me? How daring!

LADY SUSAN. Your sister takes every occasion to remind me of the lack of recreation in Churchill. Perhaps such an exercise might serve to amuse me.

REGINALD. Brilliant! Would you accompany me for a stroll about the shrubbery?

(**REGINALD** *offers* **LADY SUSAN** *his arm, which she takes as they exit.*)

CATHERINE. I cannot tolerate Reginald's presence in our home with that woman a moment longer. He is certain to fall prey to her allure.

CHARLES. I believe he has already toppled.

CATHERINE. Her behavior was appalling. In moments, she induced him to submit.

CHARLES. His submission *was* rather brisk. Why should that provoke you?

CATHERINE. You invited Lady Susan to Churchill without my knowledge, and now you expect me to stand silently by as she seduces my brother? The woman is a viper!

CHARLES. Calm yourself, Catherine.

CATHERINE. If my parents learn that Reginald has surrendered, father's delicate condition would be aggravated, and mother would be hurled into a frenzy.

CHARLES. Then surely you must keep it from them.

CATHERINE. Good God, Charles – what if he were to consider marrying her? Imagine that woman in our family!

CHARLES. She is already *in* our family.

CATHERINE. When you met with her alone, did she inquire into Vernon Castle?

CHARLES. *(Beat.)* We spoke only of Frederick. She is inconsolable.

CATHERINE. The particulars of her inheritance were not discussed?

CHARLES. They were not.

CATHERINE. I believe you are lying to me, Charles. Never before today have I suspected you of lying.

Scene Four
Evening

CATHERINE. I will not disguise my disapprobation, Reginald.

REGINALD. *(Lightly.)* You never have, sister – why begin now?

CATHERINE. The woman all but demands that you worship her. It is unseemly. She is ten years your senior.

REGINALD. You needn't worry – I can regulate my desires.

CATHERINE. When I tell mother of this, she is sure to become hysterical – and it will send father to an early grave.

REGINALD. It is hardly what one would call *early*.

CATHERINE. Do not mock me. I shall write to mother and inform her that you will be returning to Parklands at once.

REGINALD. I prefer to stay in Churchill and hunt with Charles, if you please.

CATHERINE. Reginald, get thee home!

REGINALD. *(Amused.)* Why are you so eager to be rid of me? Does my companionship no longer give you pleasure?

CATHERINE. I am revolted by your capitulation to the artifice of this unprincipled woman!

REGINALD. You are mistaken, my dear sister. Lady Susan is entirely respectable.

CATHERINE. Before you arrived at Churchill, you were decidedly against her. What has she done to overpower your reason?

REGINALD. You endeavored to *put* me against her, but I reveled in the scandalous tales. And now, having spent time with her amidst the shrubbery, I am pleased to report that I was unable to detect the smallest impropriety in her manner. She displayed nothing of vanity or pretension. Lady Susan is not at all the woman you suppose.

CATHERINE. What stronger proof of her treacherous scheme do I need than this rash perversion of judgment?

REGINALD. Not a perversion of judgment, sister – an empirical reassessment.

CATHERINE. You are deceived by the delicacy of her features – that is natural for a man. But Reginald, you must consider her behavior in town. She unfastened Sir James from Miss Manwaring – then tossed him aside like an orange peel.

REGINALD. You were misinformed, Catherine.

CATHERINE. How can you be certain? Did she provide you with the specifics of her seductions?

REGINALD. I fully intended to inquire, for sport – but we did not discuss such matters.

CATHERINE. You must await full disclosure before forming your judgment.

REGINALD. Dear Catherine, Lady Susan is altogether a wonderful woman! During our stroll, she spoke of her husband fondly, with devotion.

CATHERINE. Promise me you do not intend to marry her, for that is surely her objective.

REGINALD. Her intentions are merely those of amusement, and a desire for admiration. These are qualities I esteem in a woman, and which I am happy to indulge.

CATHERINE. *(Suspiciously.)* She inquired into Sir Reginald's health. What does that suggest?

REGINALD. That she is concerned for our father's well-being.

CATHERINE. Oh, Reginald! I am mortified to see a young man of good sense so severely duped by such a woman.

REGINALD. I am not one to be duped by *any* woman – nor am I immune to their appeal.

CATHERINE. Proceed with caution, or she will ensnare you. She will ensnare us all, unless I am able to thwart her!

WEDNESDAY

Scene Five
Afternoon

ALICIA. When Frederica showed up at my doorstep on Edward Street having been seized within hours of fleeing Miss Summer's, as Susan is my dearest friend, I knew I must deliver her daughter at once, although I am fully aware I should have stayed in town with poor Mr Johnson, who has suffered a merciless attack of the gout and is steadily deteriorating, and moreover, does not approve of my travelling without him conjoined to my side. But I knew that Susan would be eager to see for herself that Frederica was no longer at Miss Summer's, but had escaped school and rushed to my home. Is that not so, Frederica?

FREDERICA. Yes, Ma'am.

CATHERINE. Why did you flee, child? Did something occur at Miss Summer's which forced you to take flight?

ALICIA. *(Resenting the interruption.)* If you will permit me to continue – Frederica did not wish to be placed in school at all, did you, child?

FREDERICA. No, Ma'am.

LADY SUSAN. Your willingness to abandon Mr Johnson at such a critical time is most appreciated, Alicia. I am indebted to you for delivering Frederica safely to my side, where she belongs.

ALICIA. It is not the travelling that troubles me, as the roads were not rough and the balance of my curricle is superb, and though the weather did not appear unsettled, the climate is certainly no friend of mine as I am frequently assaulted by rain, putting myself at risk of a spill. Frederica, did I not invoke an acute concern that the atmosphere might turn inclement?

FREDERICA. Yes, Ma'am.

CATHERINE. You appear fretful, my dear. What troubles you?

LADY SUSAN. Since Mr Vernon's demise, the girl has rarely been in good humor.

FREDERICA. I miss Papa so.

ALICIA. The journey consumed only a few hours and the conditions did not become stormy which is to my point that it was not the travel, nay, but the destination that was not at all to my liking.

CATHERINE. The destination, you say. Do you have a particular objection to Churchill?

ALICIA. I have no opposition to your home, Mrs Vernon. I see that the furnishings are acceptable, if outmoded and ill-matched, and the drawing room is satisfactory although rather clammy, and as you are aware, I have not inspected the upstairs apartments so I can offer no criticism thither. But what I find intolerable about the country, in addition to the omnipresence of fleas and gnats, is that the very air is unsuitable for my complexion, requiring that I apply salves and unguents in an effort to maintain its natural luster. Is that not so, Susan?

LADY SUSAN. I shall take you on your word, Alicia, as I have only seen you in town, where your skin is perpetually translucent.

ALICIA. It is so. All my friends remark on it and as the doyenne of London society, they implore me to divulge my secrets, but I have always been of the mind that a woman should hold certain matters confidential, particularly those pertaining to her toilette.

CHARLES. We are delighted that you could join us, Mrs Johnson –

CATHERINE. *(Interrupting.)* – even uninvited –

CHARLES. – and as it was our fondest wish that Frederica would accompany her mother to Churchill, we are gratified you have brought her to us. Welcome to our home, child.

FREDERICA. It is a pleasure to be here, Uncle Charles.

CATHERINE. But my dear girl, are you certain you are quite well?

FREDERICA. Yes, Ma'am.

CHARLES. You can speak up, child – you are among family. You must have suffered a terrible ordeal at Miss Summer's.

REGINALD. I have heard horrid tales of boarding schools. Did something diabolic occur? Do tell!

FREDERICA. *(Noticing him, with interest.)* I am fine, sir. You needn't worry.

LADY SUSAN. Surely Frederica is exhausted from her caper, and requires rest. Come, dear. Let us withdraw to our chambers.

FREDERICA. If you please, Mama, no.

CATHERINE. You would prefer to stay with your relations, correct?

FREDERICA. Yes, Aunt.

ALICIA. This is not surprising as no sooner she was overtaken than she asked to be delivered directly to my home on Edward Street although she was in full knowledge of whither her mother was bound. Is that not so, child?

FREDERICA. It is, Ma'am.

ALICIA. And one would expect, nay, require that I should convey Frederica to Churchill as soon as humanly possible so that Susan could have no doubt as to the depth of my affection, despite the girl's strongly voiced objections which commenced as soon as we departed Edward Street, and continued ceaselessly throughout the journey with an increasing ferocity. Is that not so, child, that the clamor you generated was interminable and swelled in volume as we approached this destination, and did not subside until moments ago?

FREDERICA. I suppose, Ma'am.

CATHERINE. Her objections, you say. Lady Susan, why would your daughter object to being returned to your side?

LADY SUSAN. I myself have just learned of these circumstances, which are as astonishing to me as they are to you.

CHARLES. My dear wife, please allow Lady Susan and Frederica to confer, as mother and daughter should.

LADY SUSAN. My thanks, Charles. Come, Frederica.

FREDERICA. No, Mama.

LADY SUSAN. I insist that we remove ourselves upstairs.

FREDERICA. I should like to remain with Aunt Catherine.

CATHERINE. Where is the harm in this?

LADY SUSAN. Frederica, I must speak with you in private. Now come.

> *(***LADY SUSAN*** *takes* **FREDERICA***'s arm. Before* **FREDERICA** *leaves, she looks back at* **REGINALD.***)*

CATHERINE. She seems frightened, poor thing.

REGINALD. I find her rather unlively.

ALICIA. Mr De Courcy, you are not unworthy of the praise I have heard bestowed upon you in town. You have a fine figure.

REGINALD. That is most generous, Mrs Johnson – and entirely accurate.

ALICIA. I understand your father's estate is entailed, and you are the heir. You will be worth 10,000 a year when he perishes, will you not?

REGINALD. *(Amused.)* At the very least.

CATHERINE. I must say, any discussion of Sir Fitzwilliam's fortune whilst he is mortally ill is in questionable taste.

ALICIA. You are in error, woman. There are two crucial occasions on which to probe a man's fortune – when he is set to marry and when he has one foot in the grave. Now tell me, Mr De Courcy – have you settled on a prospect for a wife?

REGINALD. I have not. I am enjoying my bachelorhood immensely –

CHARLES. *(Approvingly.)* As are many of the young ladies hereabouts.

ALICIA. I cannot imagine there are any women with qualifying complexions to choose from in this climate. You must come to London, and I will introduce you some very lovely ladies.

CHARLES. Reginald is quite an accomplished suitor, Mrs Johnson.

CATHERINE. He is able to manage proficiently without your assistance, thank you very much.

ALICIA. That is doubtful, Mrs Vernon. My friends in town consider my intrusion in matters of courtship compulsory.

CATHERINE. Has Frederica come out in society?

ALICIA. A tolerably eligible bachelor took an interest in her, but she was repulsed by him.

CATHERINE. Who was this man, pray?

ALICIA. None of your concern. *(Continuing.)* Frederica is a peculiar girl indeed, or we would not have been forced to journey hither. Only the most extraordinary circumstance would compel me into the hinterlands.

CATHERINE. I must know the identity of this suitor!

ALICIA. I am fatigued. I should like a few words with Susan, and then I must to bed. I trust that no bats or barn owls will disturb my rest?

CHARLES. You shall not hear a sound till the gentle cooing of the mourning doves.

ALICIA. And no children, I trust?

CATHERINE. Our young son is in Parklands, substituting for Reginald with my ailing father.

ALICIA. Thank merciful God. I abhor adolescents!

(She exits.)

REGINALD. Why ever would Miss Vernon run from school? What an ungrateful child.

CATHERINE. I have my suspicions.

CHARLES. I am certain we shall hear a simple, satisfactory explanation.

CATHERINE. And I am certain you are entirely wrong.

REGINALD. Miss Vernon is exactly as I was led to expect.

CATHERINE. Led by whom, or need I ask?

REGINALD. Lady Susan shared certain remarks about her daughter as we paused near the shrubbery.

CATHERINE. What manner of remarks?

REGINALD. They were in confidence, Catherine.

CATHERINE. We are family, Reginald. Speak.

REGINALD. She informed me with great dismay that Miss Vernon was a stubborn girl and glum, who had not manners to recommend her. Having met the girl, I concur. I vastly prefer the mother.

CATHERINE. I must say I find her melancholy affecting.

CHARLES. Reginald, you have clearly misunderstood her ladyship. Frederica was a spirited child whose entire existence was overturned with her father's passing.

CATHERINE. There is a certain humility in her aspect that I find quite appealing – along with a willingness to oppose her mother.

(**LADY SUSAN** *returns, with* **FREDERICA** *in tow.*)

REGINALD. I say – look who has resurfaced!

LADY SUSAN. My apologies, but if you would all be so kind, I should like to speak with my daughter alone.

CATHERINE. *(Warily.)* The upstairs apartments offer sufficient privacy, do they not?

LADY SUSAN. As you surely observed, Alicia Johnson possesses a vivacious spirit. Moments after we entered our chambers, she burst in on Frederica and me, and despite my entreaties, could not be persuaded to leave. The woman was still chattering as we escaped down the passage.

CHARLES. Catherine, Reginald – let us withdraw to the parlour, where we shall have tea.

(**CHARLES, CATHERINE,** *and* **REGINALD** *exit.* **LADY SUSAN** *turns on* **FREDERICA.**)

LADY SUSAN. Why have you chosen to torment me?

FREDERICA. I am sorry, Mama.

LADY SUSAN. It was your advantage that led me to place you in Miss Summer's. I should be rewarded for my efforts on your behalf. Instead, I am publicly humiliated.

FREDERICA. That was not my intention.

LADY SUSAN. Why did you flee from school?

FREDERICA. I could not tolerate it a moment longer.

LADY SUSAN. You were there all of one day! And when apprehended, you asked to be taken to Alicia, who you knew full well would deliver you back to me.

FREDERICA. I feared she might, and vigorously attempted to dissuade her.

LADY SUSAN. You are a foolish girl – a consideration to which you could have attended had you remained at Miss Summer's.

FREDERICA. My education is not why you placed me there, Mama.

LADY SUSAN. It was most certainly among the reasons. I have never been so provoked in my life.

FREDERICA. I had no wish to provoke you – I merely privileged my own well-being.

LADY SUSAN. What has become of you? Before your father died, you possessed all the Vernon modesty and milkiness. But *now* look at you. I had no notion of your being such a little devil.

FREDERICA. That is ungenerous, Mama.

LADY SUSAN. Hear me, girl – you shall be punished.

FREDERICA. You never spoke to me this way when Papa was alive. What has aroused such an alteration in your manner?

LADY SUSAN.   Are you unable to comprehend that *everything* has changed – and for the worse?

FREDERICA. I am fully aware of our circumstances.

LADY SUSAN. Then you will surely grasp my motives. You shall be returned to school – your uncle has agreed to foot the expense. I will inform Alicia that you must never be admitted into her home without me again. Meanwhile, these next few days at Churchill, whilst I wait to hear from Miss Summer, whom I have implored to forgive your conduct, you are forbidden to answer any questions from your aunt. Mrs Vernon is sure to press you, but you must remain firm. And as for Reginald, if you so much as look at him, I will see to it that he is sent away.

FREDERICA. I am undeserving of this treatment.

LADY SUSAN. Frederica, your father is dead. I have no son. We have no assets. We must survive on what Charles offers, and his vengeful wife will do everything in her power to prevent him from providing us that to which we are entitled. We will likely lose the Castle. We are two women, alone, with nothing.

FREDERICA. Then why do you choose to deepen my despair?

LADY SUSAN. I am exerting all my powers to put an end to it!

FREDERICA. You and I have very different opinions on how that is best achieved, as we discussed quite heatedly in London.

LADY SUSAN. You refuse to credit that everything I have done, I have done for you. Go to bed – I've had enough of you for tonight. But hear me, girl – do exactly as I say from this moment on, or you will suffer my fury.

THURSDAY

Scene Six
Morning

SIR JAMES. As soon as I learned that you had quit town, I flew into a panic! I could not sleep a wink until I discovered your whereabouts.

LADY SUSAN. You do look a bit bedraggled, Sir James – but as determined as ever!

SIR JAMES. I thought I might never see you again. Where is her ladyship, I cried. Now I am ebullient! I am effervescent! I am – what is the word? – exasperated – is that right? I am exasperated at the sight of you! Oh, Susan! My dumpling!

> (**SIR JAMES** *runs to her, knocking aside a chair, and forcefully throws his arms around her.*)

CATHERINE. Do control yourself, sir. These furnishings are treasures.

ALICIA. At least some think so.

LADY SUSAN. *(Politely extracting herself from his clutches.)* I appreciate your exertions on my behalf, Sir James. But how did you learn whither I was bound?

SIR JAMES. Mr Johnson was kind enough to inform me.

ALICIA. *(Firmly.)* Sir James, I fully acknowledge that as my husband is in utter agony with the gout, I should be tending to his needs at this moment instead of causing detriment to my skin in this fetid swampland, but it is only proper that I support Susan, even moreso now that she is being subjected to assault. I trust you were not equally forceful with my decrepit husband who requires rest, and should not be besieged by pleas for intelligence!

CATHERINE. Bravo, Sir James! You have achieved your quest and tracked down her ladyship. However, as I cannot extend another invitation, I insist that you return to London at once.

SIR JAMES. Heavens, no! I shall remain at Churchill for several days at the very least – or longer if her ladyship will have me. I am her fervent admirer!

CATHERINE. Apparently, Mr Vernon, our home has been mistaken for an inn.

CHARLES. What a welcome relief.

CATHERINE. A relief from what, pray?

SIR JAMES. I must say, I am ravenous after the journey! I could eat a goat.

REGINALD. Regrettably, Sir James, goat is not on the menu at Churchill.

SIR JAMES. Good heavens! I have no wish to dine on billy goat – although head of ram *is* considered a delicacy in certain parts of Italy.

CATHERINE. Which is precisely why I refuse to travel.

CHARLES. I will inform cook we shall have seven for lunch.

CATHERINE. Unless anyone else is galloping in our direction.

ALICIA. I cannot imagine why Churchill is such a popular destination given the astute critiques I have offered.

REGINALD. Its current vogue is entirely attributable to Lady Susan. Multitudes are flocking here to see her!

LADY SUSAN. *(Coyly.)* Reginald, you mustn't mock me.

SIR JAMES. Mr Vernon, please inform cook that I have a hearty appetite. It has been said I eat for two!

CHARLES. I will inform cook we shall have *eight* for lunch.

CATHERINE. Sir James, why was it so urgent for you to see Lady Susan?

SIR JAMES. *(Longingly.)* I have a secret motive.

LADY SUSAN. You are a knight errant!

REGINALD. Or perhaps merely – errant.

CATHERINE. *(To* **SIR JAMES.***)* Out with it, man!

CHARLES. Catherine, desist.

SIR JAMES. Only Lady Susan shall learn of it. And now that I have voyaged to Churchill, I am entirely at her disposal.

REGINALD. It would seem her ladyship disposed of you when she departed London.

SIR JAMES. Distance is no barrier to desire, Mr De Courcy. I would follow Lady Susan to the ends of the earth!

ALICIA. You have arrived, sir.

CHARLES. Do you hunt, Sir James? Would you care to join me and Reginald this afternoon?

SIR JAMES. To hunt would require that I go out-of-doors, would it not?

REGINALD. I fear it would. My sister is disinclined to have creatures of the wild grazing on her cherished furniture.

CATHERINE. My gardens are commented upon favorably by all who behold them, Sir James – and our statuary is legendary in these parts.

SIR JAMES. I prefer to remain indoors, in the company of ladies. Ah, the ladies! Listening to them in idle chatter, or grazing – pardon – *gazing* as they float across the room sends me into paroxysms of joy.

REGINALD. Our Doctor Underwood can recommend treatment should these paroxysms prove severe.

CHARLES. Reginald, if you please.

ALICIA. It is common knowledge in London that whenever lovely ladies are present, Sir James is at fever pitch, and as a consequence, his skin becomes flushed and blotchy. Did you notice that, Frederica?

FREDERICA. I did not, Ma'am.

SIR JAMES. What an agreeable surprise to stumble upon you here, Miss Vernon. I am dumbstruck to find both mother and daughter ensconced in these remote parts. Mrs Vernon, you must be an exceptional hostess to entice the company of such fine ladies. I shall report to everyone in London!

CATHERINE. Do not, sir, I beg of you. I doubt I shall ever fully recuperate from the current stampede.

ALICIA. There can never be too many eligible bachelors, Mrs Vernon – even if they are not all as finely proportioned as Mr De Courcy.

REGINALD. I am gratified to be singled out once again for your well-observed praise.

LADY SUSAN. Sir James, would you be so kind as to accompany Frederica on a promenade about the shrubbery?

SIR JAMES. The shrubbery is situated out of doors, is it not?

CATHERINE. Of course it is, man!

SIR JAMES. Oh, blast! And are there geese about? I was once harassed by a goose. They are vile creatures – though I admit, quite delectable when roasted with turnips. I consider the turnip to be an exemplary vegetable. Does anyone agree? (*He looks about, but no one responds.*) Broccoli, perhaps?

LADY SUSAN. Frederica, taking a little turn with Sir James would be enchanting, would it not?

FREDERICA. It would not.

ALICIA. Susan, I am not unaware that her exodus from Miss Summer's was alarming, but such behavior does not require that the poor girl be hurled into the briar and bush!

SIR JAMES. Lady Susan – if you please – I would rather – that is – if I am compelled to venture al fresco, I would much prefer to promenade with you.

ALICIA. Take heed of the gnats. When I am stung, I explode!

SIR JAMES. *(Anxiously.)* Surely you don't mean explode, as in *(Makes a sound like an explosion.)* – explode?

REGINALD. I confess I am uncertain whether Doctor Underwood has a medicine for gnat stings resulting in explosions.

LADY SUSAN. I insist. Frederica, please accompany Sir James on a stroll.

FREDERICA. No, Mama.

CATHERINE. Lady Susan, it is quite clear, now as before, that Frederica prefers to stay on in the drawing room with her relations.

REGINALD. Indeed, the mere suggestion of accompanying Sir James appears to induce nausea in the girl.

SIR JAMES. But Lady Susan, I –

LADY SUSAN. *(Interrupting.)* Frederica is cautious of strangers, and has had little experience with gentlemen. She requires encouragement.

CATHERINE. This appears more prodding.

ALICIA. Often, a young girl must be spurred into considering a man she despises. The proper basis for many a successful marriage is mutual revulsion.

CHARLES. These recent months without your father have been agonizing for you, dear, have they not?

FREDERICA. They have, Uncle Charles. Truly agonizing.

SIR JAMES. If you please, Lady Susan, I have a matter I should very much like to discuss in private. It is the singular motive which hastened my journey to these far-flung environs. Would you be so kind as to accompany me into the shrubbery?

REGINALD. You mustn't venture directly *into* the shrubbery, Sir James. The popular prejudice is in favor of strolling *alongside* it.

SIR JAMES. Forgive me, sir. I am unversed in rural terminology.

REGINALD. Your safety is my sole concern, dear fellow.

SIR JAMES. I beg of you, Lady Susan – I have traversed the belly of the continent for this prospect.

LADY SUSAN. I surrender, you captivating man! Every moment alone with you is time well spent. Come, Sir James. Frederica, take heed of our discussion.

FREDERICA. I will, Mama.

SIR JAMES. And I shall work up a hearty appetite for lunch! Let's away, my muffin!

ALICIA. Beware the gnats!

> (**SIR JAMES** *offers his arm,* **LADY SUSAN** *takes it, and they exit.*)

REGINALD. *(Amused.)* One thing is certain – the man is no Solomon.

CATHERINE. Frederica, I cherish these moments in your company, without your mother's vigilant eyes boring into us.

FREDERICA. As do I.

CATHERINE. Dear niece, it is imperative that I learn what transpired at Miss Summer's school that caused you to take flight so impulsively.

FREDERICA. Alas, I have been forbidden to respond to your interrogatories.

CATHERINE. What is this?

ALICIA. Attempting to converse with Frederica can be like addressing a stone, as you have witnessed, although I prefer her reticence to these garrulous old women nowadays who blather their views gratuitously.

CHARLES. Catherine, our niece has elected not to discuss Miss Summer's school, which is her prerogative.

REGINALD. Oh, Charles – you must allow her to regale us with at least one dastardly tale!

CHARLES. All discussion on the topic of Frederica's exit from Miss Summer's will now cease.

CATHERINE. Dear niece, are you aware that you recoiled when you first saw Sir James, and your face fell?

FREDERICA. That is very likely, Aunt.

REGINALD. Her countenance *has* been rather grim since she arrived –

(**CHARLES** *signals* **REGINALD** *disapprovingly.*)

– which I attributed to her father's recent passing.

CHARLES. Catherine, you are vexing the poor girl. I insist that you conduct a less probing discourse.

CATHERINE. Half of London has descended upon my home full of secrets and subterfuge. It is my obligation to excavate these enigmas!

CHARLES. Your principal obligation to our guests is common courtesy.

REGINALD. Catherine's is a legitimate curiosity, Charles. *(Amusing himself.)* I too am eager to learn why Sir James hunted Lady Susan down, only to compel her directly into the shrubbery.

ALICIA. What is this fixation on shrubbery? Everyone in Churchill appears preoccupied with vegetation. Does no one hereabouts give a thought to fashion?

REGINALD. *(Toying with her.)* I would be overjoyed to accompany you for an amble out of doors, Mrs Johnson. Perhaps you might develop an appreciation for the wonders of nature.

ALICIA. Have you taken leave of your senses?! Nature is merely a place where cows roam about uncooked! Now Mr De Courcy, tell me more of the young ladies in these parts. Do they wear sashes and lace to hold their gowns in place, or merely buttons?

REGINALD. I am not entirely certain, Mrs Johnson, although I can state with first-hand knowledge that their apparel remains very firmly secured.

CATHERINE. Frederica, I gathered evidence that your mother pried Sir James away from his fiancée, then promptly forced –

CHARLES. *(Interrupting.)* I have had quite enough of this idle chatter for one afternoon.

ALICIA. There is nothing idle about the affairs of society, Mr Vernon. I possess all intelligence pertaining to the appetites of London's first circle, and can assure you that every morsel is worthy of consumption.

CHARLES. *(Lightly.)* I have spent my adult life secluded at Churchill, far from the grasp of good society. You must forgive me, Mrs Johnson.

ALICIA. I shall consider it.

> (**LADY SUSAN** *and* **SIR JAMES** *enter. He is scratching.)*

CATHERINE. *(Surprised.)* I must say, that was hasty. I warn you, Sir James, I will tolerate no criticism of my gardens or statuary.

CHARLES. Did you enjoy your stroll?

SIR JAMES. Not at all. I collided with an unexpected Greek, then was set upon by a swarm of gnats.

ALICIA. Do not crawl to me for sympathy, man. You were forewarned!

REGINALD. Perhaps it was your scent. May I ask what cologne you use?

SIR JAMES. Mayfair. It has a sweet floral fragrance. The ladies, I am told, find it seductive.

REGINALD. As do the gnats, apparently.

LADY SUSAN. They mistook you for an enormous flower, Sir James!

SIR JAMES. Talking of aromas, unless my nose is mistaken, we will be served lamb stew! Come, my coriander – I am famished!

(He takes **LADY SUSAN**'s *arm and hurries off.)*

CHARLES. Let us make our way to the dining room. *(Offers his arm.)* Catherine.

*(***CATHERINE*** glares at him, and after a moment, exits without taking his arm.)*

ALICIA. I require the assistance of a gentleman, if you please.

CHARLES. I am at your service, Mrs Johnson.

ALICIA. One with a formidable physique.

REGINALD. It would be my privilege to attend you, Mrs Johnson.

ALICIA. I should hope it would.

CHARLES. *(Amused.)* Come, Frederica. I trust my undistinguished anatomy is sufficient to transport you to table.

> (**FREDERICA** *takes* **CHARLES'** *arm, and they start out.* **ALICIA** *takes* **REGINALD'S** *arm, then attaches herself to his side as they start to exit.* **FREDERICA** *looks back at* **REGINALD.** *He notices.)*

Scene Seven
Afternoon

CHARLES. *(Peering out the window.)* Lady Susan and Reginald appear satisfyingly content. What an agreeable sight!

CATHERINE. *(Also looking out.)* There is nothing at all agreeable about this brazenly public display of affection.

CHARLES. Not quite public. They are well-hidden by the shrubbery.

CATHERINE. Frederica, forgive my speaking candidly, but it grieves me to see your mother, a recent widow, desperately clutching the arm of a younger man.

FREDERICA. I am also grieved, Aunt – for Reginald.

SIR JAMES. As am I – mortally, mightily, meagerly – is that the word? – meagerly grieved. Why has Lady Susan forsaken me? Have I said something to offend her? Is my cologne overpowering?

CATHERINE. Nothing is amiss with your aroma, Sir James. The woman is depraved. She devours men as if they were hot cross buns.

CHARLES. Catherine, it is barbarous of you to make ungenerous remarks about Lady Susan in the presence of her daughter.

FREDERICA. No need to refrain on my account, Uncle.

SIR JAMES. Her ladyship has always displayed tenderness toward me. Even whilst I was betrothed to Miss Manwaring, she extended a pointed hospitality in my direction.

CATHERINE. You were bamboozled, Sir James.

SIR JAMES. *(Puffed with pride.)* You are mistaken, Mrs Vernon. I always drink in moderation.

CHARLES. My dear wife, Lady Susan and Reginald are merely ambling along the shrubbery. Where is the harm?

CATHERINE. I have come to loathe the shrubbery. My garden paradise has been transformed into a den of iniquity. If someone mentions shrubbery again, I shall pull all of it out by the roots!

SIR JAMES. *(To* **CHARLES.***)* I believe you are correct, Mr Vernon. Lady Susan and Reginald are merely enjoying an innocent saunter along the shrub – *(Catches himself. To* **CATHERINE.***)* I beg your pardon, Mrs Vernon. I nearly neglected your admonition not to cite the shrub –. *(Catches himself.)*

CATHERINE. Sir James, I demand to know precisely what transpired in London when Lady Susan arrived.

SIR JAMES. Permit me to think. Ah, yes – I believe we first met at one of Mrs Johnson's receptions.

CHARLES. Talking of which, where is Mrs Johnson?

FREDERICA. *(Lightly.)* I detected what sounded not unlike a snoring bulldog as I paused on the landing.

SIR JAMES. As did I! And I was frightened for my life!

CATHERINE. We do not own a bulldog, Sir James. I will allow of no mammal to molest my furnishings.

FREDERICA. She is sleeping into the afternoon, as is her wont – to prolong her beauty rest.

CATHERINE. Mrs Johnson's whereabouts have been established. Sir James, continue.

SIR JAMES. Where was I?

CATHERINE. *(Impatiently.)* At Mrs Johnson's reception!

SIR JAMES. Ah, yes, much obliged. That evening, Mr Johnson was exhibiting gouty symptoms. Have reports of his ailment made their way to Churchill?

CATHERINE & CHARLES. They have.

CATHERINE. Returning to topic, you were in the company of Miss Manwaring when Lady Susan attended the reception, correct?

SIR JAMES. Yes, I was with my betrothed – that is to say, the woman to whom I was previously betrothed. Is there a word for that?

CATHERINE. Until Lady Susan plucked you away!

CHARLES. Catherine, do not steer the man's account to align with rumors you have engorged.

CATHERINE. Sir James, do you object to my queries?

SIR JAMES. Not at all, Mrs Vernon. As I began to say, I was with the woman to whom –. Good heavens, what is that word? I find the English language entirely deficient! Am I alone?

(No one responds.)

CATHERINE. Why are you no longer with Miss Manwaring?

SIR JAMES. Do you mean why did she not accompany me to Churchill?

CATHERINE. Yes. No. What I mean is, why are you no longer betrothed to Miss Manwaring?

CHARLES. Mrs Vernon, you are behaving like an attorney at the Old Bailey. Need I remind you that Sir James is a guest in this house?

CATHERINE. An *unsolicited* guest – and as such, I fully expect him to submit to whatever line of inquiry I impose.

CHARLES. You are stretching my patience, woman. Let us direct the discourse to something more agreeable, shall we? Sir James, Reginald shot a few pheasant on our hunt. They will be served for dinner, roasted and wrapped in sage!

SIR JAMES. I rather wish you had kept that knowledge from me, Mr Vernon. It agitates my digestion to be reminded that something on my plate was quite recently alive. What will be served for dessert? I trust that Reginald did not shoot the dessert.

CATHERINE. Did Lady Susan arouse your desires so that she might –

SIR JAMES. *(Interrupting, to* **CHARLES.***)* Shrewsbury cakes, perhaps? I do love Shrewsbury cake. And I adore those little pink cakes with seeds in them. What are they called? Someone? Anyone?

CATHERINE. Sir James, I am convinced that you have no useful information whatever to offer.

CHARLES. Which mercifully concludes this discussion.

CATHERINE. Hold your tongue. Frederica, the time has come for you to respond.

FREDERICA. I beg you to recall, Aunt Catherine, that I have been forbidden to answer any inquiries from you.

SIR JAMES. Why in heavens would you be forbidden to answer questions from your dear aunt?

CHARLES. I can conceive of many reasons.

CATHERINE. You have nothing to fear in answering, Frederica.

FREDERICA. I am not fearful, Aunt – I am forbidden.

SIR JAMES. Who on God's green turf has forbidden you?

FREDERICA. I am disinclined to say.

CATHERINE. Only one person would stoop to such an injunction, Sir James.

SIR JAMES. I am surely no ignoramus, but I lack the vaguest notion of who might forbid Miss Vernon from responding to your queries.

CATHERINE. Frederica, as your beloved relation, I demand that you put all prohibitions to one side, and comply with my entreaty.

CHARLES. Catherine – restrain yourself.

FREDERICA. I am sorry, Aunt Catherine, Uncle Charles. I do not wish to be the cause of marital dispute.

CHARLES. You are hardly the cause, Frederica. At the moment, you are merely the conduit.

FREDERICA. Nonetheless, it pains me to be implicated.

CATHERINE. I am convinced that your deposit at Miss Summer's somehow involved Sir James. Is that not so?

SIR JAMES. What is this? Am I involved? Am I – implicated?

CATHERINE. Frederica, I insist that you respond!

CHARLES. And I insist that you cease this line of questioning at once.

FREDERICA. My dear Uncle, I have not been forbidden from answering any questions that Sir James might pose.

SIR JAMES. *(Pleased.)* Good fortune indeed. You will find that I am conversant on many topics.

CATHERINE. Brilliant. Sir James, please repeat the question I asked of Frederica.

CHARLES. *(Annoyed.)* This puts me in mind of a game I played as a child.

SIR JAMES. Let me think. The conversation has been so topsy-turvy, I have quite forgotten. We were discussing little pink cakes, and then –

FREDERICA. *(Interrupting.)* She asked if you were somehow involved in my banishment to Miss Summer's.

SIR JAMES. Ah, yes, that was it. Very good.

FREDERICA. And the simple fact is, it was Mama who –

CHARLES. *(Interrupting.)* I have had entirely enough of this inquisition!

CATHERINE. Muzzle it, Charles! We are on the brink of discovery!

CHARLES. Mrs Vernon, hold your tongue. Frederica, Sir James, if you would repair to the parlour, I should like to speak to Mrs Vernon alone.

SIR JAMES. Of course. Miss Vernon, may I accompany you?

(Offers his arm.)

FREDERICA. No, sir. Go on ahead, if you please.

SIR JAMES. Very well. As you say. *(Glances out the window.)* Oh Susan! My sweetmeat! Will you return to my arms, or have I lost you for all eternity? I am in agonies!

(Exits.)

FREDERICA. Dear Uncle Charles. Kindest Aunt Catherine. You have been exceedingly generous since my arrival, and I am grateful to you for all the courtesies you have extended. I offer my deepest –

(Exits.)

CHARLES. Catherine, your behavior is appalling. I can tolerate a degree of meddling, given the lack of amusement in Churchill. But I will not permit this relentless interrogation of our guests. You are intrusive and impolite, and I shall no longer abide this conduct from my wife, in my home.

CATHERINE. You are blind, Charles. Like your brother, you refuse to acknowledge what is glaringly apparent. Lady Susan is a selfish, manipulative woman who will trample anyone in her path to achieve her ends. She jeopardized our marriage, vanquished Miss Manwaring, manipulated Sir James, imprisoned her own daughter, and now, as we speak, she is furthering her crusade to ambush my brother! I warn you, husband – open your eyes before it is too late!

Scene Eight
Evening

(FREDERICA waits anxiously. After a few moments, she sees someone enter an offstage room.)

FREDERICA. *(Whispering, loudly.)* Mr De Courcy!

REGINALD. *(Hearing FREDERICA, he enters.)* Good evening, Miss Vernon. You appear anxious.

FREDERICA. Please excuse this liberty, sir, but I am forced upon it by great distress, or I should be ashamed to trouble you.

REGINALD. No need for apology. What pains you?

FREDERICA. I am very miserable about Sir James Martin.

REGINALD. He *is* a bit of a rattle, but you mustn't allow him to ruffle your feathers. I find him quite entertaining, actually.

FREDERICA. I have no other way of helping myself but to speak with you privately.

REGINALD. I am happy to oblige, and I assure you our communication is in confidence. Yet I fail to grasp why I have been selected for this surreptitious exchange, as holding a secret is not among my virtues.

FREDERICA. I have observed that you enjoy a particular fondness for mother.

REGINALD. We met just days ago, and within moments, I capitulated! *(Catching himself.)* I am discomfited, however, to learn that my particular fondness, as you say, is so transparent.

FREDERICA. I beg you, sir – persuade her to abandon her intention to have me wed Sir James.

REGINALD. Surely you are mistaken, Miss Vernon. It is evident that Sir James has planted his affections quite firmly with your mother.

FREDERICA. She has no interest in him save as husband for me. She removed him from Miss Manwaring with the sole design of steering him in my direction. And I cannot bear the sight of him.

REGINALD. There, there. If you inform her of your true feelings, she will happily release you from this arrangement you are persuaded she desires.

FREDERICA. She is fully aware of my true feelings, sir. We argued forcefully on the subject in London.

REGINALD. I am perplexed. She is not an unreasonable woman.

FREDERICA. I understand how highly you esteem her, sir, but I am quite certain of her intentions.

REGINALD. Surely Sir James would not surrender to this strategy.

FREDERICA. Mama is unyielding, and singular of purpose. But if you will employ the great kindness I am certain you possess to take my part and convince Mama to dismiss Sir James, I shall be eternally indebted. So long as he remains at Churchill, she will attempt to force him upon me. You have already witnessed her efforts to this end, and my resolute refusal to participate in her scheme.

REGINALD. Indeed, I confess I was puzzled when you rebuffed your mother's harmless request to accompany Sir James on a stroll.

FREDERICA. You do not understand me, sir. This is not a sudden fancy. I found him silly and disagreeable and impertinent in town, and since his arrival in Churchill, my distaste has intensified.

REGINALD. Silly to be sure, and arguably disagreeable, but hardly impertinent. You judge him too severely, Miss Vernon. You must reconsider your mother's sensible effort to find you a suitable husband. As a man of wealth and rank, Sir James is a worthy, if – unusual suitor.

FREDERICA. I would rather work for my bread than marry him.

REGINALD. Oh my. Work, you say. That *is* excessive. I see now how resolved you are in this matter. You have placed me in an awkward position, Miss Vernon. As a man with a deep fondness for your mother, I do not wish to incur her animosity.

FREDERICA. I have taken great liberty in speaking with you, and I am aware how dreadfully angry it will make her. I acknowledge the risk, but it is commensurate with the loathing I feel for the man I will be forced to wed unless you intervene. You have a tender soul, sir. I can see it in your eyes – and I feel it in my heart.

> (**FREDERICA** *looks longingly into* **REGINALD***'s eyes. The sound of footsteps.* **FREDERICA** *peers offstage.*)

Mama is coming!

> (*She hurries out from the other side of the drawing room as* **LADY SUSAN** *enters.*)

REGINALD. Lady Susan, may we speak a moment?

LADY SUSAN. Certainly, Reginald.

REGINALD. Your daughter is suffering under a severe misapprehension.

LADY SUSAN. (*Displeased.*) You have been speaking with Frederica?

REGINALD. She took me aside in confidence.

LADY SUSAN. I had mentioned that her manners are wanting, and now you have proof.

REGINALD. The girl is convinced that you wish for her to marry Sir James. I disputed her claim, as it is glaringly apparent that the man is besotted with you. Yet she implored me to intervene.

LADY SUSAN. Intervene in what way?

REGINALD. Simply put, she would very much like for you to send Sir James packing.

LADY SUSAN. She has behaved foolishly. I promise you she shall be disciplined.

REGINALD. No need of that.

LADY SUSAN. It was inappropriate of her to importune you, a stranger, and entirely improper to request that you intercede. I apologize, on her behalf.

REGINALD. You are aware, are you not, that the poor girl despises Sir James?

LADY SUSAN. She expressed that opinion to me privately, and now she has chosen to publish it.

REGINALD. Surely you would not force her to wed a man she loathes.

LADY SUSAN. Reginald, you cannot fathom the sacrifices I have made for this ungrateful girl, yet she continues to defy me.

REGINALD. It wounds me to hear you speak this way, Lady Susan.

LADY SUSAN. You have been coerced into a situation which is none of your concern. You should have refused her application to mediate.

REGINALD. I was convinced that she misunderstood your intentions. I assumed the matter would be easily resolved. I see now I was wrong. I was also mistaken in my judgment of you.

LADY SUSAN. Whatever do you mean?

REGINALD. I believed you to be a virtuous woman, but as the mother of a frightened child, your behavior is nothing short of tyrannical. I shall take my leave of you at once.

    (He starts out.)

LADY SUSAN. Reginald, I beg of you. Permit me to explain.

REGINALD. There is no excuse you could offer. We view the world differently. I am of the mind that every person's wishes, even those of a young girl, should be given consideration. Yet you treat her cruelly. Your daughter is in torment, and you are the cause.

LADY SUSAN. Reginald, please hear me. Since I lost my husband, I have been entirely devoted to Frederica. My sole desire is for her to be in possession of a fortunate establishment when she is wed. I make no apologies for that – it is also what her father wished. Sir James is a man of amiable disposition and excellent character, and in every respect, a good match for the girl. That is the reason I encourage her to consider him. It is all I ask. To hear you render these fierce and unrestrained remarks against my character wounds me, sir. I have come to care for you deeply in the brief time since we have met. Your sudden disregard for me is the cruelest of blows. What can I do to redeem myself in your eyes – and in your heart?

REGINALD. You can consider your daughter's pleas.

LADY SUSAN. I will do that, for you.

REGINALD. And you can say it is me you love, and not my fortune.

LADY SUSAN. Oh Reginald! I can live without money, but I cannot live without love!

REGINALD. *(Rushes to her side, and falls to his knees.)* My dearest, dearest woman. I have misjudged you. I shall never again doubt a word you say!

> (**REGINALD** *takes* **LADY SUSAN** *in his arms, and they kiss.* **FREDERICA** *peers in and stares.)*

ACT II
FRIDAY

Scene Nine
Evening

(Can be performed without an intermission.)

LADY SUSAN. Within moments, Reginald was at my feet, begging forgiveness. Then he graced me with a kiss!

ALICIA. You are the most consummate actress in England. Not even Sarah Siddons, whom I saw in *Macbeth* at Drury Lane, could compete with your artfulness.

LADY SUSAN. *(Lightly.)* I've always had a particular fondness for Lady Macbeth.

ALICIA. While I have no patience for a woman so ill-equipped at performing her toilette that she is incapable of removing spots from her own hands.

LADY SUSAN. To dislodge a self-assured young man from his pedestal offers endless delight.

ALICIA. I am quite smitten with Reginald. He is a delicious flirt with a magnificent shape!

LADY SUSAN. The man provides much needed distraction in this suffocating home. But I have more serious matters to attend. First, I must attach Sir James to my daughter. I had resolved to return her to Miss Summer's, but when he surfaced, I saw how I could spur my plan into immediate action.

ALICIA. With your scheming, I trow they shall be wed within weeks, although the man is utterly dimwitted and will likely walk down the aisle uncertain of whom he is to espouse, fixed instead on the wedding feast.

LADY SUSAN. He proposed marriage on our stroll along the shrubbery, Alicia. I averred that as a recent widow, it would be improper to wed so soon. But I must keep him on a leash. Frederica is intractable, and I am in a prickly position. It shames me to confess it, but in a world where a widow without a son cannot inherit wealth or property, what am I to do but seduce and scheme?

ALICIA. I rank those skills highly. A learned lady is easily ignored, but no one neglects an accomplished seductress.

LADY SUSAN. No man, at least. Women are more discriminating. Mrs Vernon is a she-wolf who has become rabid in her campaign to turn Charles against me. I was privy to numerous accounts of her petty, malevolent disposition before she and Mr Vernon were wed. As a dear friend, I cautioned him of the misery he would endure were they to marry, and begged him to throw her off – to no avail.

ALICIA. Now the poor man is enmeshed in her clutches forever, amidst these abhorred furnishings.

LADY SUSAN. I must be on guard not to unnerve him. I am confident Charles will restore Vernon Castle to my possession, if only to spite his wife.

ALICIA. I am convinced he detests Mrs Vernon, and rightly so. She is a meddlesome creature with deplorable taste.

LADY SUSAN. It pains me to disparage our sex, Alicia, but I prefer men – they are easier to manipulate. An obstinate daughter and a malicious sister-in-law – why am I so plagued? This predicament requires the vigorous employ of all my talents. Only then shall I return to town triumphant. Ah, London! Why ever did I leave?

ALICIA. Need I remind you?

LADY SUSAN. I did nothing that should arouse such tumult. Miss Manwaring is a vapid creature, and Sir James was eager to be rid of her.

ALICIA. She continues to pine for him – thinner than a walking stick, and pale as a phantom. She has taken to bed like a consumptive heroine in a bad play.

LADY SUSAN. Sir James is no longer hers. The sooner Mrs Manwaring launches the hunt for another son-in-law, the sooner Miss Manwaring's complexion will be restored.

ALICIA. Despite the endless application of emollients, her skin was never among the most radiant in town, a condition which she attempted to disguise by putting her mother to quite an expense in beauty patches and vegetable rouge.

LADY SUSAN. Alicia, when we return to London, might Frederica and I reside with you on Edward Street? To be sure, we are no longer welcome at the Manwarings.

ALICIA. That will not be possible.

LADY SUSAN. Why ever not?

ALICIA. Mr Johnson will not have it.

LADY SUSAN. What has he to do with it?

ALICIA. It is his home.

LADY SUSAN. He is bedridden. You have many rooms. We will keep well out of his way, I assure you.

ALICIA. Susan, I must inform you – indeed, I rushed to Churchill expressly to notify you that Mr and Mrs Manwaring were at our doorstep moments after you left.

LADY SUSAN. I see. So that is the reason you have come.

ALICIA. It is for you and you alone that I was compelled into this primeval thicket!

LADY SUSAN. I presume the Marnwarings did not loiter on your doorstep?

ALICIA. Indeed not. Mrs Manwaring stormed inside and engulfed my husband in sorrowful tales of her family's despair as a direct result of your improprieties. Mr Johnson is enraged at the torment you have caused, as the Manwarings are his dearest friends.

LADY SUSAN. And what of *Mr* Manwaring?

ALICIA. He waited in the parlour till Mr Johnson sent for him, whereupon, he informed my husband that he was in love with you, and intended to separate from his wife, who began to weep voluminously.

LADY SUSAN. *(Beat, then lightly.)* Silly man. Before I left town, I asked him to wait until I returned, when we would consider these matters together.

ALICIA. You kept this from me, Susan. I assumed the conquest was for sport.

LADY SUSAN. It was, at first. But to my surprise, I developed a genuine fondness for him.

ALICIA. I soon as I met him, I presumed that your interest had turned toward Mr De Courcy. His musculature is triumphant, and soon, he will come into considerable wealth.

LADY SUSAN. I enjoy Reginald, to be sure – but Manwaring is utterly his superior.

ALICIA. Society will not allow it.

LADY SUSAN. Society be damned.

ALICIA. Susan! To toy with a married man is one matter, but to speak ill of society is quite another. I shall not have it.

LADY SUSAN. It is Mr Manwaring I want, Alicia, and Mr Manwaring I shall have.

ALICIA. I am pained to inform you that I was forced to promise Mr Johnson I would never allow you into our home again. Should I disobey, he threatened to desert London, and remove us to the country for the rest of our days. I was thrown into a panic! I could never survive such an extremity. Marooned in some festering cesspit for all eternity? Never. Even if it costs our friendship.

LADY SUSAN. Surely you can convince your husband of the depth of our devotion, and the genuineness of my request.

ALICIA. Mr Johnson has been murderously violated by the gout! I refuse to prod him into his tomb with postulations and pleas.

LADY SUSAN. The man has been infirm for far too long, Alicia. He should make a decision whether he prefers to live or die.

ALICIA. That is heartless.

LADY SUSAN. Confess it – you are eager to be rid of him.

ALICIA. I have never uttered such a thing!

LADY SUSAN. Your conduct has consistently revealed it.

ALICIA. That is an entirely different matter.

LADY SUSAN. You abandon him when he is most in need, and then prolong your stay in Churchill.

ALICIA. I came to deliver an errant daughter – and to convey these portentous developments!

LADY SUSAN. Which you should have divulged the moment you arrived. But at present, you could best assist me by overruling your husband's command.

ALICIA. And be condemned to rusticate?! Never!

LADY SUSAN. Where ever shall I lodge when I return to town?

ALICIA. In one of the unfashionable districts. You are no longer welcome in good society.

LADY SUSAN. I have misjudged our friendship. I was foolish to place my trust in a garrulous old woman.

ALICIA. I am not garrulous – I am forthcoming And I am not old – I am – seasoned! Adieu.

Scene Ten
Evening

REGINALD. You appear distraught, dear friend.

ALICIA. I have been too long without society. I pine for the metropolis! You must come to town more often, Mr De Courcy. I shall invite you to one of my balls, where you will behold the most bewitching ladies in all of England. A man worth more than 10,000 a year should not mummify himself in this quagmire.

REGINALD. That is most kind, Mrs Johnson. I rarely visit London, and when I do, I remain for but a few days on father's business before I scurry home to the company of the less significant ladies hereabouts.

ALICIA. You would marvel at what the women in society are wearing nowadays. They follow the French fashions. Their attire is almost sinful.

REGINALD. My interest is piqued, Mrs Johnson. Please tell me more of these immoral garments.

ALICIA. The necklines plunge exceedingly low, and the soft, muslin dresses cling to their bodies.

REGINALD. I accept your offer! I shall attend one of your receptions when I am next in town. Although at present, I must remain with father.

ALICIA. How fortunate that the renowned Reginald De Courcy chose to vacate Parklands this week that I might at last have the chance to meet him.

REGINALD. Ours is an acquaintance that is sure to thrive, Mrs Johnson. I enjoy your company exceedingly. You speak with admirable candor.

ALICIA. My friends always credit my frankness, save when they dispute my judgments.

REGINALD. Let me state unequivocally that whether I accept or challenge your opinions, I support your willingness to expound them.

ALICIA. Very astute. It is a rare man indeed who surpasses his reputation, Mr De Courcy. Yet I question why a superior gentleman such as yourself would forsake the paterfamilias in his hour of need.

REGINALD. I confess I could not resist the chance to lay my eyes upon the woman around whom so many rumors swirled.

ALICIA. *(Disapprovingly.)* As I suspected.

REGINALD. My sister assailed me with unending tales of her ladyship's improper conduct, however, as is often the case, Catherine was utterly mistaken.

ALICIA. Susan has beguiled you, Mr De Courcy, as she has various men these many months, with her husband not yet cold in the ground.

REGINALD. I proudly proclaim I am smitten with this tempting armful!

ALICIA. My husband would surely challenge such accolades.

REGINALD. Mr Johnson is not susceptible to her ladyship's charms?

ALICIA. I must be discreet. Do I have your word that any intimacies I unveil are in strictest confidence?

REGINALD. I shall not betray your trust.

ALICIA. Permit me to journey back through time.

REGINALD. I am your eager companion.

ALICIA. When her husband perished and she materialized in London, Susan immediately demanded my friendship. I generously took it upon myself to introduce her into the best society. I disclosed that

Sir James, though conspicuously deficient in various aspects, was quite prosperous. Promptly, she tore him from Miss Manwaring, while Mrs Manwaring was already in the midst of momentous discussions with the milliners. Are you aware of the latest trends in millinery, Mr De Courcy?

REGINALD. I am not. Continue.

ALICIA. We have progressed from simple bonnets to styles that are wider in size, and increasingly ornate, with –

REGINALD. *(Interrupting.)* Continue with your account of Lady Susan, if you please.

ALICIA. I shall. As soon as the wedding was quashed, she foisted Sir James upon Frederica.

REGINALD. I heard tell of this.

ALICIA. And being stupid as a stump, Sir James was unaware that Susan had now directed her attentions toward Mr Manwaring –

REGINALD. *(Interrupting.)* Mr Manwaring?! I had not heard tell of *this*.

ALICIA. Vigorously she beset him, an exploit which did not go unnoticed by his wife, who was already distraught, as in an effort to lure Sir James, she had spent a fortune on ball gowns for her daughter, all of which, to my mind, displayed a deplorable lack of satin.

REGINALD. I cannot believe what I am hearing!

ALICIA. I am an expert in the field! If you choose to disparage my fashion sense, I shall assemble all my acquaintances to testify on my behalf.

REGINALD. I have no doubt your fashion sense is unassailable, Mrs Johnson. Go on.

ALICIA. Promptly, with my encouragement, the first circle shunned her.

REGINALD. *Your* encouragement, you say?

ALICIA. As is only proper. The woman is unfit for society. Whereupon Susan fled town, chucked her daughter into school, then scurried hither to escape the malicious talk which had begun to flood the city, pour into the provinces, and dribble down to your ears.

REGINALD. You weave a remarkable narrative, Mrs Johnson.

ALICIA. I am renowned for my oratory.

REGINALD. The reports were true!

ALICIA. Every word – and more.

REGINALD. Mrs Johnson, you have spoken kindly of Lady Susan this past week. What instigated you to turn so forcefully against her?

ALICIA. The woman disparaged me!

REGINALD. I cannot imagine a living creature who would do such a thing – apart from my sister. Whatever did she say?

ALICIA. You would never suppose it, but Susan finds me garrulous. I am hardly garrulous, sir. I am a woman of few words, and disperse my syllables sparingly.

REGINALD. Indeed, your discourse is never voluble – and always valuable.

ALICIA. She also alleged that I am old. I am not old, Mr De Courcy, nay – I have yet to reach my summit.

REGINALD. You are vaulting ever upward!

ALICIA. What is worse, Mr Johnson has threatened our expulsion to the savage wilds if I do not terminate my friendship with Susan. The very notion repulses me as you may be aware from a few veiled remarks I have volunteered these many days.

REGINALD. Mrs Johnson, I must leave.

(Starts out.)

ALICIA. Just one moment, sir. I have something more that will be of interest to you. But keep hold of your pledge, Mr De Courcy – not a word!

Scene Eleven
Evening

REGINALD. You yanked Sir James from Miss Manwaring, then you –

LADY SUSAN. *(Interrupting.)* Sir James caught my eye at Alicia's reception, and *he* approached *me*. Apparently, his intentions did not extend to marriage.

REGINALD. They were engaged!

LADY SUSAN. I had no idea at the time. You attribute more powers to me than I possess. May I ask why you've suddenly elected to credit false reports you previously dismissed? Has Mrs Vernon finally managed to turn you against me?

REGINALD. Once you pried Sir James from his betrothed, you set him upon Frederica, then imprisoned her in school, but no sooner was she entombed than she bravely –

LADY SUSAN. *(Interrupting.)* Imprisoned? Entombed? Really, Reginald. Many young girls detest school. Frederica is not unique. She is resolute – a trait I value in her. Have you have spoken again with my daughter?

REGINALD. Why should I allow your interpretation when you condemned Frederica for merely confiding in me? I was a fool to believe you!

LADY SUSAN. What in heavens has caused this sudden tear in your feelings toward me?

REGINALD. As if the utter ruination of Miss Manwaring was not enough, you proceeded to entrap *Mr* Manwaring!

LADY SUSAN. Ah, I see. You have visited with Mrs Johnson.

REGINALD. And regretfully, I am breaking my promise to her by speaking with you. Have you no shame for all for the misery you have caused?

LADY SUSAN. I explained to Mrs Manwaring that despite my valiant attempt to restrain him, the entire time I was in residence at their home, her husband was in hot pursuit of me. When she was not persuaded, I chose to leave London.

REGINALD. Society abhors you! Admit to it – you were expelled!

LADY SUSAN. The situation became intolerable, what with Miss Manwaring whimpering, Mrs Manwaring blubbering, and Mr Manwaring chasing me like a determined hound. That is when I wrote Charles and accepted his offer to visit.

REGINALD. Do you suppose that I would take your word over Mrs Johnson's?

LADY SUSAN. I spoke unwisely in my conversation with Alicia. I fed her gossip to quench her desire for it. It was a performance. That is what women do – it is the weakness of our sex. Little of what I said was true, and you should not believe a word of it. Mrs Johnson's motives are entirely selfish. I believe she wants you for herself.

REGINALD. That is absurd. She is a married woman.

LADY SUSAN. Who very soon will be a widow like me.

REGINALD. Lady Susan, you have destroyed the Manwarings, repulsed Mr Johnson, mocked your dearest friend – and now, you have lost Mr Manwaring.

LADY SUSAN. What is this?

REGINALD. He returned to his wife, whom he married for her wealth. His only interest in you was your fortune. When he learned from Mr Johnson that you were destitute, he was quick to discard you and return to the arms of his moneyed wife. So much for your celebrated skills as a seductress. You are unloved, abandoned and insolvent – which is precisely what you deserve.

LADY SUSAN. Reginald, that is unkind.

REGINALD. I am candid.

LADY SUSAN. *(Beat, as she considers her options.)* Which is one of the qualities I most admire in you. From the moment you arrived in Churchill, I could see that you were an exemplary man. I savored your companionship, and in these few days, I've grown increasingly fond of you. I hoped you might feel the same toward me. We even shared a kiss.

REGINALD. It revolts me to think how readily I succumbed to your deceit. I thought myself a promising flirt, but I am no match for you – nor do I hope to be.

LADY SUSAN. If I behaved poorly, I am deserving of your censure. But my feelings for you are genuine, Reginald. I ask you to believe that. I can do no more. Please forgive me, I beg of you.

REGINALD. Do not attempt to seduce me again, Lady Susan. You will fail.

LADY SUSAN. I have no desire to seduce you, sir. My only wish is that you fathom my plight. To that end, I shall be as frank with you as you have been with me. I am a widow, in inferior circumstances, in need of an advantageous marriage. You are an admired bachelor, the representative of an ancient family and heir to the estate. I do not presume myself to be the only woman you might consider for a wife, but I am not unaware that I possess many attributes which qualify me an attractive companion for a man such as yourself.

REGINALD. Are you suggesting I could best serve your needs by replenishing your resources? How venal!

LADY SUSAN. I said I would be forthright. I hoped you would value that.

REGINALD. And what of me? What do I acquire in exchange? A bauble on my arm?

LADY SUSAN. We are alike in many ways, Reginald. We both possess the skill to captivate.

REGINALD. I have no interest in such a negotiation, woman. You are unworthy. You bewitched me, but now the spell is broken. My only wish is that Frederica is not made to suffer a moment longer!

(He storms off.)

SATURDAY

Scene Twelve
Evening

LADY SUSAN. We are undone. We have nothing – and you are entirely to blame.

FREDERICA. Papa died and we lost everything. How am I at fault?

LADY SUSAN. I extended every effort to find you a suitable husband in Sir James, and you behave as if the sheep were a wolf.

FREDERICA. I do not wish to marry a sheep.

LADY SUSAN. We are without a shilling. Vernon Castle is your dowry, and as you refuse to marry Sir James, we are without a roof.

FREDERICA. I care nothing for the Castle. True affection is the most valuable dowry.

LADY SUSAN. You do not possess the luxury to marry for love.

FREDERICA. I refuse to marry a man for whom I lack tender devotion.

LADY SUSAN. And you will suffer for it. We will both suffer. What have you to offer? You are not a handsome girl.

FREDERICA. That is beneath you, Mama.

LADY SUSAN. I do not hold it against you, Frederica – but it is precisely why you were placed in Miss Summer's. How do you expect to acquire accomplishments?

FREDERICA. In London, while you were otherwise engaged with Mr Manwaring, Mr Johnson sent me to a bookshop in Finsbury Square with instructions to purchase whatever I wished. I procured *The Wrongs of Woman* by Mary Wollstonecraft, an anthology of poetry, and *Fables of la Fontaine*, by which I taught myself rudimentary French. You underestimate me. I have no need to attend school – I have learned from you.

LADY SUSAN. You learned none of that from me.

FREDERICA. Your example taught me how to make use of the skills I possess.

LADY SUSAN. Which skills, exactly, provoked you to escape from Miss Summer's? It was a perverse and willful act.

FREDERICA. You perceive any action of mine that does not correspond to your wishes as perverse and willful.

LADY SUSAN. You are a child, Frederica. You do not have a say in the choices I make for you.

FREDERICA. I am no longer a child, Mama. You have neglected to notice.

LADY SUSAN. I noticed that you made an effort to attract Reginald's attention.

FREDERICA. And you were jealous of me, which fueled your rage.

LADY SUSAN. I will not compete with my own child for the attentions of any man!

FREDERICA. You would prefer to impel me into a marriage with a man I despise.

LADY SUSAN. For you own benefit.

FREDERICA. How could a life of unhappiness be beneficial?

LADY SUSAN. What do you know of life?

FREDERICA. Very little indeed, but enough to know I shall not be forced to do what I oppose, even by an adversary as formidable as yourself.

LADY SUSAN. As long as you are dependent on me for your survival, you will do as I say.

FREDERICA. I am sorry, Mama, but I will not. When I am trapped, I will fight to escape. *That* I also learned from you. I applied to Reginald, hoping he might convince you of the error you were making, to which you had become blind in your reckless effort to secure position. He was the one man I believed could influence you.

LADY SUSAN. You targeted him purposefully to provoke me.

FREDERICA. I did not, Mama. But I had grown fond of him. *(Beat.)* When he was present, I experienced sensations I had never known.

LADY SUSAN. I cannot believe what I am hearing. Who is this stranger speaking to me?

FREDERICA. We have more in common than you suspect. I am a woman like you.

LADY SUSAN. You are not a woman as yet. You are a girl, and my daughter. Had I a son and an heir, I would not be in the position I am in.

FREDERICA. Mama, I beg you to check your impulse to strike when circumstances do not suit you. Papa would disapprove. Such behavior will only lead to suffering and strife, as you experienced in London, and here again at Churchill.

LADY SUSAN. You have been speaking with your uncle and aunt. What do you know of their intentions for Vernon Castle?

FREDERICA. Nothing. And I have managed to honor your request to ignore Aunt Catherine's inquiries. But understand this, Mama – while Uncle Charles is predisposed to assist us, your rash impulses have made that less likely. This intemperate behavior and affinity for manipulation are not worth the cost. We would both be better served if you behaved with courtesy and moderation. I beg you to take heed.

LADY SUSAN. Who are you to advise me?

FREDERICA. These are the teachings and the conduct I learned from Papa.

> *(Beat.)*

LADY SUSAN. Oh, Frederick. *(She turns away. After a few moments, tenderly.)* Come. Sit by me, Frederica.

SUNDAY

Scene Thirteen
Morning

ALICIA. Although I cannot claim that I have enjoyed one moment of my visit to Churchill even remotely, and it is unlikely that my complexion will ever fully recover, I am obliged to thank you for your hospitality, Mr Vernon. You are not discourteous, and the food has been tolerable.

CHARLES. I shall accept that as a compliment, Mrs Johnson. Your visit has been our good fortune, and you are welcome at Churchill any time.

ALICIA. That is a very generous, if entirely unnecessary offer. I cannot imagine the circumstances which would necessitate a return to this stagnant hellhole – *(To* **REGINALD.***)* unless I violate Mr Johnson's prohibition.

CATHERINE. What prohibition is this?

ALICIA. None of your concern.

REGINALD. This is not the last you will see of me, Mrs Johnson. I shall accept your invitation to town. I long to witness those handsome ladies in revealing garments.

CATHERINE. I am encouraged that you have not attached yourself exclusively to Lady Susan, Reginald. And now, you must proceed homeward. I shall inform mother, who has likely become deranged. I have neglected my duty to write to her for days now, having been preoccupied with surveilling this procession of guests through my once tranquil abode.

CHARLES. *(Lightly.)* When you were not preoccupied with prying into their affairs.

FREDERICA. *(Entering from upstairs, happily.)* Good morning, all.

CHARLES. Good morning, niece. I must say, you possess a glow this morning.

FREDERICA. It is a glorious day, is it not?

CATHERINE. And what makes this day unlike any other, pray?

ALICIA. You are relieved to learn of my departure, is that it? How barbaric.

FREDERICA. I treasure your company, Mrs Johnson, as I trust you are aware.

ALICIA. I require more reminders, child.

FREDERICA. Then you shall have them.

*(**FREDERICA** hugs **ALICIA**, startling her.)*

ALICIA. What is this onslaught of affection? Unfasten yourself!

CHARLES. I trust Lady Susan will be joining us for breakfast, Frederica?

FREDERICA. Mama is preparing for our removal. We shall return to London today.

CHARLES. This is sudden. I presume from your good spirits that this withdrawal is not the consequence of any predicament for you or your mother.

FREDERICA. Quite the reverse.

CATHERINE. I must say I am astonished. I fully expected these intruders to tarry for months.

ALICIA. You cannot demand our company forever. I am a fiercely devoted wife with a husband who has been pulverized by the gout!

REGINALD. I am grieved to see you depart, Mrs Johnson. As for Lady Susan, I am thankful to be rid of her.

CATHERINE. Reginald, do my ears play me tricks? You are elated that her ladyship is leaving Churchill?

REGINALD. I should have heeded your warnings, sister. She is precisely the woman you feared, and I was blind to it.

CATHERINE. There, you see Charles? *(To* **REGINALD.***)* And how did you arrive at this inevitable conclusion, pray?

CHARLES. Rein it in, Catherine. Your wish has been granted – let that suffice.

ALICIA. I am puzzled by Susan's sudden leave-taking. Reginald, I fear you neglected to keep your promise.

REGINALD. You are quite right, Mrs Johnson. I behaved impetuously. You must forgive me.

ALICIA. *(Coyly.)* Of course.

CATHERINE. What promise?

ALICIA. Keep to your business, woman.

FREDERICA. On behalf of my mother, I should very much like to apologize to everyone present for any distress she might have caused. I beg of you all – do not think harshly of her.

CHARLES. How very thoughtful, Frederica.

REGINALD. I must say, it has been a tumultuous week, and I am eager to return home. "Happy the man whose wish and care a few paternal acres bound, Content to breathe his native air, In his own ground."

FREDERICA. I adore Alexander Pope!

REGINALD. Brilliant! Perhaps we might we read together in these remaining hours of each other's company.

FREDERICA. I should enjoy that, Mr De Courcy. Truth be told, I am saddened to leave Churchill. I feel quite at home here, and whilst I have yet to step out-of-doors, I am quite certain I would enjoy the country air.

REGINALD. How satisfying to see you so buoyant. I had begun to think despondency was your natural state.

FREDERICA. Today I feel a burden has been lifted.

CATHERINE. Entirely too many secrets are underfoot this morning for my liking. Mrs Johnson's decision to depart, a prohibition imposed upon her, Frederica's abrupt change of attitude, she and her mother's return to London, Reginald's startling rebuke of Lady Susan, a promise he made to Mrs Johnson, and a mysterious burden, suddenly lifted. As mistress of Churchill, I demand answers!

ALICIA. You'll worm nothing out of me, rustic!

FREDERICA. Nor do I have any desire to review the events that have transpired. It is a new morning, the sky is bright, and I am refreshed. If you please, Aunt Catherine, I prefer to revel in the sensation rather than explain how it came to pass.

CHARLES. Well circumvented, Frederica.

REGINALD. *(To* **FREDERICA***.)* I too feel somehow liberated, although I was unable to yield fully to my own joy until I beheld yours.

FREDERICA. I am pleased to have been of assistance, Mr De Courcy. Now would you be so kind as to accompany me for a stroll through the oft-mentioned shrubbery?

REGINALD. I would be charmed.

ALICIA. Do either of you care nothing of gnats?!

> *(***FREDERICA*** offers her arm.* **REGINALD** *takes it, and they exit.)*

CATHERINE. This is more than I could have hoped. What have I done to deserve such good fortune?

ALICIA. Not a thing.

CHARLES. The girl is transformed. It is remarkable.

CATHERINE. Lady Susan will be mortified to see Frederica prancing about the shrubbery with Reginald. The chickens have come home to roost!

CHARLES. Do not gloat, Catherine. It does not sit well on your features.

(**LADY SUSAN** *enters from upstairs.*)

LADY SUSAN. Good day, all. What a fine morning!

CHARLES. Frederica was only just commenting on it.

LADY SUSAN. Where is my daughter, pray?

CATHERINE. She is just outside, about the shrubbery – with Reginald, if you please.

LADY SUSAN. How delightful! I must say, those paths have been well-trod this week past. If shrubbery could talk, what secrets their branches might divulge.

CHARLES. Frederica is very gay this morning, Susan.

LADY SUSAN. As am I – gay as a lark. We have all been so engrossed in our affairs these many days that we have denied ourselves the occasion to be festive. What fools we mortals be.

CATHERINE. She informed us that you are departing for London.

ALICIA. I am astonished at this sudden leave-taking, Susan. After our tête-à-tête, I supposed that you would linger on indefinitely in this squalid cavity. Where will you reside in town?

LADY SUSAN. I have heard of some lovely apartments on Upper Seymour Street.

ALICIA. Upper Seymour? On which side of the street?

LADY SUSAN. The fashionable side.

ALICIA. However shall you bear the expense of a residence there?

LADY SUSAN. I intend to stop by Miss Summer's and request a reimbursement on payment I had made for Frederica's tenure.

CHARLES. My niece will not return to school?

LADY SUSAN. Frederica and I had a long-overdue conversation last evening. I have been so distracted since her father's demise that I have neglected the girl's needs. We sat side by side, mother and daughter, well into the night, and spoke of many things. We agreed that Miss Summer's school was not the place for her, and decided to return to London together.

CHARLES. *(To* **CATHERINE.***)* The riddle of the lifted burden has been solved.

LADY SUSAN. I have imposed on your hospitality for too long, Mrs Vernon.

CATHERINE. You will hear no argument from me on that point. I am eager to resume the serene existence I led before this tumult. I am, after all, a simple woman.

ALICIA. That is indisputable.

LADY SUSAN. *(Hearing the sound of footsteps.)* You are not rid of all of your guests just yet, I fear.

*(***SIR JAMES** *enters from upstairs.)*

CHARLES. Good day, Sir James.

LADY SUSAN. How lovely to see you. But you look a bit queasy. Did you sleep well?

SIR JAMES. Not at all. The worrisome quantity of oysters that I ate with dinner last night provoked an insurrection in my stomach.

CHARLES. I shall ask cook to prepare a cup of clear broth.

SIR JAMES. *(Sniffing.)* Do I smell sausages? There is nothing quite like the aroma of pig-meat in the morning! When

I suffer from indigestion, a big, bountiful meal is just the thing to reinvigorate me!

LADY SUSAN. Sir James, I must inform you that I am quitting Churchill, and returning to town.

SIR JAMES. Oh, my, this is abrupt. What did I do to offend? Tell me, I beseech you!

LADY SUSAN. Nary a thing. However the time has come to turn the page – and bring down the curtain.

SIR JAMES. But – I voyaged to Churchill to capture you and you alone, my pancake.

LADY SUSAN. And I am delighted you did, Sir James. I enjoy your attention immensely.

SIR JAMES. But – what I mean is – what am I to do now?

LADY SUSAN.   Just this moment, when I saw you approaching, I thought to myself, "I should very much like to ride to town with Sir James Martin in his barouche. In the case of inclement weather, I am in sure hands with such a fine man." Does that suit you, sir?

SIR JAMES. Nothing would suit me more! I am delightedly, deliriously, delusionally – is that the word? – delusionally happy!

> (*He runs to* **LADY SUSAN**, *knocking aside a chair, and forcefully throws his arms around her. She extracts herself.*)

CATHERINE.   (*Wounded.*) Sir James, that chair is undeserving of your brutality!

ALICIA.   (*Approvingly.*) My, my Susan – how very resourceful you are.

CATHERINE. I demand an explanation for that cryptic remark.

ALICIA. It was not offered for your elucidation.

LADY SUSAN. Dear Alicia, you are welcome to visit my lodgings whenever you like.

ALICIA. I fear when I return to town, I shall have no time for society until Mr Johnson is in his grave – at which point, I look forward to welcoming you once again into society!

LADY SUSAN. We shall resume our friendship with the same intimacy as ever, dear friend.

CATHERINE. More subterfuge! I must know what has transpired under my roof to bring about these peculiar transformations.

ALICIA. I have had quite enough of you this morning.

CATHERINE. That was an impertinent remark, Mrs Johnson.

ALICIA. It was intended as such.

> (**FREDERICA** *and* **REGINALD** *enter. They are arm in arm, enjoying each other's company.* **LADY SUSAN** *and* **CATHERINE** *notice, and are pleased.*)

FREDERICA. Good morning, Mama.

LADY SUSAN. Good morning, darling.

CHARLES. Did you enjoy your walk?

FREDERICA. Very much, Uncle. The country air suits me.

CATHERINE. Were the gardens and statuary to your liking?

FREDERICA. They are lovely, dear Aunt.

REGINALD. And what of your companion?

FREDERICA. He is also quite suitable.

CATHERINE. Frederica, why rush to London so soon? You are more than welcome to remain with us at Churchill for as long as you wish.

FREDERICA. That is ever so charitable, Aunt Catherine.

CHARLES. If your mother approves.

LADY SUSAN. Yours is a generous offer, Catherine – and it appears nothing would please Reginald more.

REGINALD. *(Warily.)* You are a fortunate woman indeed to have such a remarkable daughter, Lady Susan. I trust you appreciate that.

LADY SUSAN. I do, Reginald. Truly I do. My life has been an unending trial of late, and I have not always behaved in a manner of which I am proud. I know that you, Charles, have perceived my follies and offenses these many days, for which I offer my humblest apologies.

CHARLES. Your missteps are entirely attributable to the dire situation in which you have have been placed since my brother's demise.

LADY SUSAN. When I see Frederica on Reginald's arm, it is undeniable that my daughter has managed to rise above my failings. She is a clever young woman who does me credit. I am in raptures that she will enjoy the company of such a fine gentleman as yourself, Reginald.

REGINALD. Lady Susan, you are an extraordinary woman!

ALICIA. I see two marriages in the near future and though the men are not equally alluring, they are both rich, which is all that matters.

CATHERINE. Marriages? You are putting the carriage before the horse, Mrs Johnson.

ALICIA. Hush, woman! I shall not be hindered from ventilating my views!

CHARLES. Susan, this hurried departure has not allowed us the opportunity to settle Frederick's estate. Might we discuss the matter before you depart, or shall I plan a visit to town?

LADY SUSAN. As for myself, Charles, I desire nothing. I should like that whatever you and Mrs Vernon choose to provide is bestowed entirely upon Frederica.

FREDERICA. Oh, Mama!

*(***LADY SUSAN** *and* **FREDERICA** *embrace.)*

CHARLES. And may I ask – what of Vernon Castle?

LADY SUSAN. Nothing would bring me more joy than for the Castle to be bequeathed to my daughter.

CATHERINE. She shall have it when she is wed, as Inheritance law requires.

CHARLES. Blast Inheritance law! I shall give the Castle to Frederica whenever she wishes – right this moment, if it would please her! That is my decision, Mrs Vernon, and I shall brook no discussion on the topic. *(To* **FREDERICA**.*)* Vernon Castle is yours, my dear.

FREDERICA. *(She embraces him.)* Thank you ever so, Uncle! Papa would be grateful.

LADY SUSAN. He would indeed. You are all he could have wished for, dear daughter.

FREDERICA. *(Noticing* **CATHERINE**'*s displeasure.)* I should like for you to visit Vernon Castle as often as you wish, dear Aunt.

CATHERINE. That is most kind – and quite appropriate.

SIR JAMES. I must eat! Come, my giblet – to the pork!

LADY SUSAN. I must keep a close eye on you, sir, so that your stomach does not incur another insurrection.

CHARLES. You shall be busy as a bee, monitoring Sir James' appetites, dear Susan.

LADY SUSAN. When a woman can't obtain what she desires, she must settle for whatever she acquires.

*(***LADY SUSAN** *and* **SIR JAMES** *exit.)*

REGINALD. How shall we entertain ourselves this afternoon, Frederica, when we've finished reading?

FREDERICA. I wish to pick a few flowers and catch some butterflies. Then I should like to hunt with you, Reginald.

REGINALD. Hunt, you say. How very strange, for a girl.

FREDERICA. *(Proudly.)* I am a strange girl indeed!

> (**FREDERICA** *offers her arm.* **REGINALD,** *amused, takes it, and they exit into the dining room.)*

CATHERINE. Just as suddenly as they arrived, our guests are dashing off without a by-your-leave. How very rude.

CHARLES. I believe they have kept you satisfyingly occupied this week, although you would never acknowledge it. *(Lightly.)* Shall I send out more invitations?

CATHERINE. Not while there is breath in my body.

CHARLES. You have my word, dear wife.

> (*He kisses her cheek, with affection.)*

ALICIA. Am I expected to hobble to the dining room unattended?

CHARLES. I am at your service, Mrs Johnson – if you will have me.

ALICIA. You will suffice.

> (**CHARLES** *offers* **ALICIA** *his arm, and they exit.* **CATHERINE** *stands, empty and alone a few moments, then* **FREDERICA** *returns.)*

FREDERICA. Aunt Catherine, please – come sit by me!

CATHERINE. Nothing would satisfy me more, child. During the meal, I should like to share several ideas I have on furnishings for Vernon Castle.

(**FREDERICA** *takes* **CATHERINE***'s arm, and* **CATHERINE** *smiles, as they exit.*)

The End

www.ingramcontent.com/pod-product-compliance
Lightning Source LLC
Chambersburg PA
CBHW071929130726
47909CB00014B/2786